Alistair Highet

Stories of Robin Hood

By the same authors in Piccolo

The Obstinate Ghost and Other Stories
Ghosts Go Haunting
A Brew of Witchcraft

Geoffrey Palmer and Noel Lloyd

Stories of

ROBIN HOOD

illustrated by Derek Stenberg

A Piccolo original
Pan Books London and Sydney

First published 1976 by Pan Books Ltd,
Cavaye Place, London SW10 9PG
© Geoffrey Palmer and Noel Lloyd 1976
ISBN 0 330 24641 0
Printed and bound in Great Britain by
Richard Clay (The Chaucer Press) Ltd, Bungay, Suffolk

Contents

for Derek and Fred

Introduction

Was Robin Hood a real person, living in Sherwood Forest and leading a band of outlaws? Nobody knows for sure. Some people think he is just a character in medieval ballads, or a memory of forest fairy beliefs, or a figure representing many men who lived outside the law. The first mention of Robin Hood in literature is in William Langland's *The Vision of Piers Plowman*, which was written in 1377. The oldest ballad we have about him, called *Lytell Geste of Robyn Hode and his Meiny*, dates only from the fifteenth century; so it is not surprising that actual facts are few and fancies plentiful.

There are now so many stories about Robin Hood, and so many places associated with him, that it is not likely that the question of his existence will ever be proved one way or the other. It is certain, though, that he will always be the ideal hero for everybody who enjoys tales of courage and adventure, of rebellion against injustice, and of right overcoming wrong.

If Robin Hood did live, who was he? Why did he become an outlaw? Very little is known of his early life. There are several accounts which do not agree with each other, but the most likely one is that he was born at Loxley in Nottinghamshire (though no trace of that village remains today) in about 1160 in the reign of

Henry II. His exploits as an outlaw took place during the reign of Richard I, and he died while Henry III was king.

His real name was Robert Fitzooth, and his father was a nobleman. When he was a young man he was wild and reckless, and so extravagant that he soon spent all the money his father had left him and fell heavily into debt. Then, either because his creditors were after him, or because he grew tired of his way of life, he decided to take refuge in the forests which then covered large tracts of the north of England.

Gradually he gathered around him about a hundred men, all of whom had good reason to leave their own homes. Chief among them were Little John, Will Stutely, Will Scarlet, Much the miller's son, and Friar Tuck, a monk who had quarrelled with his order. (Maid Marian, who appears in some of the stories, was first mentioned in a ballad printed soon after 1500, and it is possible that she was only a character in a May Day play or Morris Dance. She appears for the first time with Robin Hood in a play of 1601.)

In those far-off days the game and forest laws were severe and unpopular. All deer belonged to the king, and the forests were supervised by a Warden, with foresters-at-fee acting as policemen. Forest courts were held at which cases of poaching and tree-felling were heard, and punishments were harsh. A man could have his right hand cut off, his eyes put out, or he could be executed. The serfs in England were poor and oppressed, and many could not resist the temptation to kill a deer to provide food for their families, but they always took grave risks. In the England of Robin Hood a man could hardly call his soul his own, unless he were of noble birth or a freeman owning his own land. Many of them were forced to flee from the law and hide in the dense forests, where they lived by killing deer and robbing unwary travellers.

Robin Hood was an outlaw who was different from most. He was generous to the poor, a champion of justice, cheerful and brave, and would never harm a woman. He was a happy-go-lucky thief who was loved by all who suffered under the rule of the barons. Even some of the bishops and wealthy merchants he robbed fell under his spell, as they were often given a good feast after their purses had been taken from them. Robin's chief enemy was the Sheriff of Nottingham, whom he tricked several times, and who was never able to capture him. Robin was especially hard on church-men who sided with the rich and lawyers who made money from the poor.

The life of the outlaws was hard and dangerous. It was not always summer in Sherwood Forest, and con-ditions in the bitter weather of winter could not have been pleasant. But it was a free life, full of adventure and excitement.

Robin is said to have lived in the forest until he was an old man, except for a break during which he entered the service of King Richard and fought with him both at home and abroad. When he became ill and was no longer able to bear the hardships of an outlaw's life he went to Kirklees Abbey near Huddersfield to get medical help from the Prioress, who was his cousin, and with whom he thought he would be safe.

But the Prioress betrayed his trust, and brought about his death by opening an artery in his arm and locking him in a small room to bleed to death. 'Bleeding' was the usual cure for many ailments in those days, so there was nothing suspicious about the treatment.

After Robin's death the stories of his exploits were passed from person to person by word of mouth for a long time before the ballad-makers heard of them. They developed and enlarged them, and added bits of older stories. Robin Hood's fame grew and spread and he eventually became the folk hero of the common people. Such he has remained ever since.

Robin Hood and Little John

On a spring morning in Sherwood Forest when a warm wind was stirring the young leaves of the oak and birch trees, and birds were singing of a world turning green, Robin Hood arose from his bracken bed in the forest glade. The quiet days he and his men had spent for many weeks had grown tedious to his adventurous spirit and he felt restless. The need for action tugged at him. He washed his hands and face in the cold water of a little brook that trickled by the outlaws' camp, and shook the sleep from him. Then he slung his quiver over his shoulder and took up his bow.

'I feel a stirring in the blood,' he said to Will Stutely, one of his closest friends among the outlaws, 'and I am going to the edge of the forest to see if there is adventure about. I want you and the rest of the men to stay here, but be sure you remain within earshot of my horn call in case I need you. If you hear three blasts, come quickly.'

'You may be sure of that, master,' said Will. 'We have plenty to do here, but we shall look forward to your return.'

Robin made his way through the dense forest, his feet treading lightly on the springy turf. His heart lightened as his keen eyes took in the blue sky above flecked with wisps of cloud, and below the scutter of white tails as rabbits lolloped away into the under-growth, and as he heard the shrill cry of a jay and the chatter of starlings. A squirrel gave him a beady glance as it scuttled up a tree, and in the distance a deer ran like a brown ghost and vanished behind a clump of trees. An early butterfly flew past his face and made him blink.

'This is the life,' he thought contentedly. 'I shall never understand how people can live in towns amid noise and bustle.'

Near the forest edge he took a narrow sandy path that dipped towards a broad stream chuckling over smooth speckled stones. The only way to get across it was by way of a wide tree trunk that spanned the two banks. The makeshift bridge was slippery and uneven and anyone crossing it had to be sure-footed. Robin stepped on to the tree trunk and swayed for a moment before gaining his balance. He took a couple of steps forward then stopped in surprise.

Approaching him from the other end of the bridge, and also a little way along it, was a man who must have been at least seven feet tall. He was broad-shouldered, fair-haired, and had a bearded weather-beaten face. In one hand he carried a blackthorn staff. The two men glared at each other. Then they both advanced, almost meeting in the middle of the bridge, eye to eye, chest to chest, though Robin had to tip his head backwards to look up at the stranger, who was fully eight inches taller than he was.

'Stand aside, fellow,' Robin said in a tone that showed he was a leader of men, 'or go back, I do not mind which.'

The man gave a short laugh. 'Who are you to tell me what to do? I will only give way to a man better than myself.'

Robin felt his anger rising. None of his men would have dared to speak to him like that. 'You will soon see who is the better man. Take care that you do not get an arrow through your ribs. Then you would pitch into the stream and the water would close your insolent mouth for good.'

'You are talking like a coward,' the man said. 'It is easy to make such a threat when you can see that I do not carry a bow.'

'Coward!' Robin gasped. 'Do you know who you are talking to?'

'I do not care who you are,' the man retorted. 'I only know that a man with a bow who threatens another who carries only a staff must be a coward. I only fight fairly, bow against bow, staff against staff, fist against fist.'

Robin was stung by the taunt, for no one before had ever accused him of being unfair. 'Then it shall be staff against staff,' he said coldly. 'Stay here until I arm myself with such another branch as you have, and we shall soon see who shall cross the bridge first. Do not go away,' he added, moving off, 'or I shall call "Coward" after you!'

'Fear not,' was the reply. 'I will be here when you return.'

Robin made his way back to the bank, where he cut himself a staff of ground oak, about six feet long, and hastily trimmed away the twigs. As he was doing so he heard the stranger whistling, and looked at him out of the corner of his eye. 'He is the tallest and biggest man I have ever seen,' he thought, 'and if his muscles are as hard as his body then I shall have a hard fight on my hands.' But his slight unease did not show as he regained his position on the bridge.

'I am ready,' he said. 'I will teach you as much about quarter-play as I could about archery. The one who tumbles in the water first is the loser.'

'That suits me,' the man declared. 'What a tune I am going to play on your ribs!' He began to twirl his staff above his head. Then he called, 'One, two—'

'Three!' Robin roared and made a feint which caused the stranger to hesitate for a moment. Robin swung his staff with such force at his opponent's head that, if it had met its mark, the fight would have ended there and then. But the stranger turned the blow skilfully and in return gave one so violent that it would have felled Robin immediately if he had not swerved an inch to one side as it landed, and it was the edge of his shoulder that was grazed rather than his head.

Robin lunged again and his staff thudded against the stranger's ribs. 'Keep at it, little one,' the man grunted. 'The fight has only just begun. I am but warming up. Look to your head!'

But Robin managed to duck in time and heard the whistling sound the blackthorn made as it slashed through the air. He shook the hair out of his eyes and prepared to retaliate.

Backwards and forwards on the narrow bridge the two men fought, for what seemed an age to both of them. They grew red-faced and breathless, each determined not to give in, though each felt an increasing admiration for the other's skill and courage. Occasionally Robin gave a cry of pain or the stranger a groan as blows were given and received, but most of the time the mighty forward thrusts of the tall man were countered by Robin's swift undercuts. They were equally matched and there seemed no reason why the parry, thrust and blow should ever end.

Then the stranger suddenly stepped forward with a furious onslaught, intent on finishing off the impudent young man who had kept him hard at it for such a long time. But Robin, dodging the blows, sprung in swiftly and unexpectedly and landed such a blow on the ribs that the man staggered and came within an inch of falling into the water.

'By my life, you can certainly hit hard,' he gasped, and while he was staggering back to his feet his staff swung round and caught Robin off his guard. Robin gave a yelp, his feet slid from under him, and he toppled head over heels into the water with a great splash.

The stranger roared with laughter. 'Where are you now, good lad?' he shouted.

Robin reappeared, his head and shoulders dripping. He felt no ill-will towards his opponent for it had been a fair fight, and the funny side of the situation struck him. 'I'm in the flood and floating down with the tide,' he spluttered. 'I shall be lucky if I don't get carried out to sea!' Gaining his feet, he started to wade to the bank, though his progress was slowed down by the slimy water weeds that clung round his legs.

'Let me help to fish you out,' the stranger said, still laughing, and held out his huge hand.

Robin seized it gratefully and was hauled up on to the bank, where he lay panting like a stranded fish. Soon the dizziness left him, though his head was still aching. He touched the sore place tenderly. 'My head is humming like a hive of bees on a summer day,' he said ruefully. 'I have never met such a fighter with the staff in all my life. I give you best.'

'It was a good fight,' said the man, 'and you have taken your beating bravely, like a hero. You put me in mind of a man who lives hereabouts, who they say is as brave as a lion and cunning as a fox. Maybe you have heard of him? Robin Hood is his name.'

Robin gave him a quick look but did not answer. Instead, he took his hunting horn from his belt and

blew three blasts on it that went echoing among the forest trees.

'Why did you do that?' asked the stranger.

'You will soon see,' Robin replied, and fell silent.

It was not long before a rustling of leaves and cracking of twigs announced that they were no longer to be alone. The stranger looked up in surprise and a little alarm when the sounds grew nearer, and when twenty or so men, all dressed in Lincoln green, burst into view, with fierce-looking Will Stutely leading them, he jumped to his feet, seized his quarter-staff, and prepared himself for battle.

The outlaws closed round the two men, and Will Stutely took in Robin's bedraggled appearance. 'How is this, master?' he cried. 'You are wet from head to foot.'

'Yes,' said Robin. 'I have just received a beating from this fellow and he tumbled me neck and crop into the water.'

'Then he shall himself receive what he gave you!' cried the hasty-tempered Will. 'First a beating, then a ducking! Have at him, lads!'

The outlaws leapt at the stranger, but they found him so ready to defend himself, striking out on all sides with his staff, that a number of them had to rub their heads and nurse their ribs. But they managed at last to hold him so tightly that he could not get away, then they carried him to the water's edge and heaved him right into midstream.

Robin ran to the bridge and mockingly inquired, 'And where are you now, my fine friend?'

A vigorous splashing was the only answer. The

stranger took Robin's outstretched hand and hauled himself up beside him. He was quivering with anger and glared furiously at the laughing men on the bank. 'Come,' he cried, 'I will take you one at a time, three at a time, even five at a time if you like, but no man makes a fool out of me!' He moved towards them.

Robin placed a restraining hand on his arm. 'But you made a fool out of me!' he said. 'Friend, let us have no more fighting. We have both got wet but let our wits be dry.'

'Very well,' the stranger agreed, a little doubtfully. 'After all, I did knock you into the water first. But who are you, and who are these men?'

'First tell me who you are,' said Robin.

'My name is John Naylor, and I come from Mansfield,' the big man said. 'In the town they call me John the Little because I am the tallest man for miles around.'

'And what are you doing in the forest?' Robin asked. 'We are more than a league from Mansfield. Have you lost your way?'

'No,' said John the Little shortly. 'I worked for Ralph of Mansfield, who is the cruellest master between here and York. Yesterday morning I slept too late, and he ordered me to receive forty lashes of his longest whip. But I did not like the idea, and I broke the head of the fellow who was set to guard me. So I thought it best to leave the town quickly, having no wish to end up on the gallows. I am seeking Robin Hood. I want to put my hand in his and be his man.'

Robin held out his hand. 'Then put your hand in mine,' he said.

John the Little stared at him. 'You – a youngster – you are this Robin whom men will live and die for, so they say?'

'I am the same Robin, and I am looking for men to live for me. Will you join my band?' Robin pointed to the outlaws, who were listening with interest to what was going on. 'Here are some of them. Will Stutely is the fellow with the quick temper, but he means no harm and has a good wit. I can promise you three suits a year and a share in whatever happens to us, good or bad. There will be venison to eat and the best ale to drink. And you shall be my right-hand man, for never have I seen such a cudgel player.'

John shot out his hand and engulfed Robin's in his broad palm. 'I am your man,' he said simply.

Then Will Stutely shook the new recruit by the hand, and the other outlaws followed suit, one by one. The tension had gone, and a feeling of relief brought laughter and good-humoured jokes. Turning their backs on the stream, they returned through the forest to their chief hiding-place. John the Little saw huts built of bark and branches of trees, and couches of rushes and bracken covered with the skins of fallow deer. Beneath a great oak tree was a seat of green moss, and Robin sat down on it. The rest of the band straggled into the clearing in twos and threes, and one group had with them a couple of fat does. They began to roast the animals over a great fire and opened a barrel of ale.

When the feast was ready they all sat down around Robin. Will Stutely was at his left hand, and Robin beckoned to John to sit at his right.

'Before we eat, master,' Will said, 'there is something we must do.'

'What is that, Will?' said Robin.

'Why, we must christen the new infant in our household, this bonny baby who is so small that his old name will no longer serve him. John Naylor – John the Little – I will be your godfather.' He picked up a pot of ale and held it over John's head. 'From now on your name will be Little John and you will serve Robin Hood faithfully for the rest of your life.' He slowly tipped over the pot.

'That I will,' said Little John, with brown ale streaming over his head and trickling from his nose and bearded chin. 'I do not remember the first time I was christened, but I will never forget the second! Now I will christen myself,' and he took the pot and poured the rest of the ale down his throat.

Robin Hood seized a portion of venison and stuffed it into his mouth. 'I am well pleased with this day's adventure,' he mumbled. 'A sore head and sore ribs will heal, but it is not every day that one can find a recruit as stout of bone and true of heart as Little John.'

Butcher for a day

One day Robin decided that the time had come for another adventure. Life had been good in the forest during the long summer days, but now he had grown weary of the shooting contests, the wrestling and other sports with which he and his men had spent their time. For a long while he had not heard what the Sheriff of Nottingham, his sworn enemy, had been up to. A trip into Nottingham might be interesting, he thought. Anything might happen … So he took his staff, made his way to the forest edge, and was soon strolling along the road to Nottingham.

For a while nobody came in sight, and it was as if he were the only living thing abroad on this fine, warm day. Then, about half a mile away, from round a bend in the road, there appeared a horse-drawn cart with, it seemed, only one occupant. Robin withdrew behind a tree and waited until the cart was level with him. He saw that it was being driven by a hearty-looking young man who was singing at the top of his voice, and the pleasure he was getting out of his efforts more than made up for the lack of tune and rhythm. The cart itself was laden with large cuts of meat.

Robin stepped from his hiding-place. 'Good morrow, friend,' he called. 'I envy you your happiness, even if I do not recognize your song!'

The man reined his horse to a halt. 'Good morrow to you, stranger. Who would not be happy on a day like this? The sun is warm to my back, I have health in my body, and there is all this fresh-killed meat in the cart that I hope to sell in the market.'

'All good reasons, friend,' said Robin. 'It is meet to have meat to sell.'

'It is also meet to have meat to meet my quarter's rent,' the young man grinned back. 'It would be meeter still if I knew your name.'

'Men call me Robin Hood.'

A shadow passed over the young butcher's face. 'Robin Hood from Sherwood Forest? I have heard of you – what do you want of me? I have hurt nobody – I am an honest tradesman.'

'Honest tradesmen have nothing to fear from me,' said Robin, a plan forming in his mind. 'As to what I want from you – are you going to the market at Nottingham?'

'I am.'

'And the meat you are taking – what price will it fetch? No, stay, what price would you put on your meat, your horse and your cart?'

'Why, sir, I had not thought of selling my horse and cart. I need them for my weekly visit to the market.'

'Come, butcher, think about it now. What price would give you such a profit that you could buy another horse and cart?'

The butcher scratched his head. This was the strangest thing that had ever happened to him. 'I'd say – ten pounds would be a good price, taking into account the cost of living—'

Robin interrupted him. 'Ten pounds, you say?' He fumbled in the purse at his belt. 'I'll give you twelve, to include your shirt and apron. And you shall have my shirt – and the advice to hurry home as a shirt of Lincoln green is not looked upon with favour by the King's foresters!'

The butcher jumped down from his cart and hastily removed his apron and shirt. 'Done, Robin Hood. I accept your generous offer. I can do with the extra money, for I am soon to be married to the fairest lass in Ollerton.'

'I wish you much happiness,' said Robin, 'and I hope you will go on singing.' He took off his own shirt and handed it to the butcher. 'Wish me luck too, for I am to be butcher for a day in Nottingham market.'

'That I will, honest Robin,' said the butcher, looking at the coins that Robin had put in his hand.

'There are many who would not agree with that description! Farewell.' Robin hoisted himself up on the driving seat, took up the reins and drove off to the town, leaving the young butcher to trudge back home on foot, well pleased with his morning's business.

When Robin got to Nottingham he made for the market-place and the special part where the butchers gathered. He greeted the men who were already setting up their stalls, found an empty space, and in a short time was ready for business. Then it dawned on him that he had no idea what he should charge for the meat. He wondered whether to ask his fellow traders what they were asking, but decided that he would make his own prices and thus be sure of selling all his stock. After

all, he was not out to make money, but to enjoy the new experience and see whether it would lead to anything more exciting. Picking up a long knife and stout cleaver he banged them together, making such a noise that people strolling nearby stopped and gathered round his stall.

'Come along, good people! Come buy from me! Fine meat for a penny, and worth all of three!'

He began to do brisk business, much to the disgust of the other butchers, and his stock dwindled quickly.

'Only a penny for a juicy steak!' he called. 'And maybe a pretty maid will seal the bargain with a kiss!'

Many maidens, shopping for their mothers or mistresses, were glad to give a kiss to this handsome butcher. But Robin's generosity did not stop there. He would not accept even a penny from the poor and elderly, but pressed the meat in their hands and was content with a blessing.

When a fat priest approached, penny in hand, Robin frowned at him. 'I am sorry, father, but the price has just gone up. The smallest piece will cost you sixpence, and a larger one a shilling.'

'Rogue,' said the priest, 'I shall go elsewhere to buy.'

'Do so, father, then my price can go back to a penny. By the look of you, you are not starving.'

The other butchers were having a very lean time. They started to grumble among themselves, wondering who this odd newcomer was, and whether he would appear every week to ruin their business.

'He must be a fool to sell for so little,' said one of them. 'He can be making no profit at all.'

'He's a thief, I'll be bound,' said another. 'I expect he stole that horse and cart and all the meat in it.'

'Not so,' objected a third. 'What thief would part with his ill-gotten gains so cheaply? At the prices he is charging it would not be worth his while. I expect he is just a novice who has no idea how to run his business.'

'Then he must be a rich novice,' said the first butcher, 'and we must not be too hasty in running him down. There might be more meat where the first lot came from, and we might well have a share in it. Suppose he owns a lot of cattle—'

'And land—' said the second.

'And a purse fuller than ours will ever be … I think we should make his acquaintance,' said the third.

They all agreed that such a move might be to their benefit, and when Robin's stock was all sold, they crowded round him. 'You have had a good day's trading, I see,' said their spokesman.

'I have indeed,' said Robin, smiling broadly. 'I am sorry that there is nothing left to sell to you!'

'We have enough meat left of our own, thanks to you,' the butcher said, a sour note creeping into his voice. 'But, as a fellow tradesman, we invite you to join the Butchers' Guild. Today we are to dine with the Sheriff at the Guildhall. Each Guild is asked in turn, and today it is ours. It will be a magnificent feast, for the Sheriff does not spare any expense.'

'I am not surprised,' thought Robin, 'seeing that the money comes from the people of Nottingham.' Aloud he said, 'Very well, brothers, I will join you with pleasure.' The occasion would be a test of his disguise, if nothing else, he decided.

He left his horse and cart in the charge of a friendly ostler and made his way with his fellow butchers to the Guildhall.

The Sheriff had already been told of the strange behaviour of the new butcher, and when Robin entered the hall one of his nobles pointed him out. The Sheriff gave the newcomer a brief glance. 'So that is the fellow who sold his meat for a penny a piece?'

'That is he, sire.'

'And who accepted kisses in part payment? And sometimes gave it away free?'

The Sheriff sniffed. 'He must be a fool indeed to throw his money about so wantonly.' Then he thought to himself, 'But if money is to be thrown, then I will make sure that some of it comes in my direction.'

He sent a servant to ask Robin to join him at the head of the table, and Robin, quaking a little inside, for he had not thought that he would have to be so close to the Sheriff, took the seat he was shown to. But the Sheriff seemed to have no suspicion that his guest was other than he seemed to be. 'I hear that you are a merry fellow,' he said. 'Will you now say grace so that we may begin?'

'With pleasure,' said Robin. He stood up and recited:

'Pray Heaven bless us all,
  And our meat within this place;
  And sack so good to warm our blood,
  And thus I end my grace.'

'Well said,' the Sheriff remarked. 'Short, and to the point.'

'Sire,' said Robin, willing to play the part of a rich young spendthrift that seemed to have been thrust upon him, 'to show how I appreciate the honour of dining with you, will you allow me to pay for the wine that is drunk here today?'

'No, no,' protested the Sheriff, 'this is my feast, and I will settle the account. You spend your money freely, young man. I think you must have much to spend. Are you wealthy?'

'In a way,' said Robin. 'My brothers and I have many a head of horned beasts.'

'How many?' The Sheriff leaned forward, suddenly very interested.

'Four hundred – five hundred – perhaps more. I do not know exactly.'

'Have you much land too?'

'A couple of hundred acres – again I am not sure. I have never asked my steward to measure it.'

'Then why should a rich man like you come to market and sell his meat so cheaply?'

'Alas, sire,' said Robin, putting on a grave face, 'owning beasts and land is all very well, but we need money, and my brothers and I have not been able to sell a single head of cattle recently. Nobody has the money in these hard times to pay the price I ask. Selling my meat so cheaply was really a gesture of despair.'

The Sheriff's eyes lit up. Surely here was a chance to trick this foolish young man into parting with his beasts for a very small sum. 'I am sorry to hear of your trouble, good fellow, but perhaps I may be able to help. I might consider buying your beasts. What do you want for them?'

'Five hundred pounds would be a fair price, I think,' said Robin.

The Sheriff stroked his beard. It was indeed a fair price. Half as much again would not be overcharging, but he was determined to pay much less. 'Nay,' he said, 'you would never get that price for four hundred beasts, even from the King himself. What about three hundred? I would willingly pay that, even though I could get cattle at a lesser price elsewhere. What do you say to three hundred pounds?'

Robin sighed. 'You strike a hard bargain, sire. But we need the money quickly and cannot wait for a better offer.'

'Good. Bring your herd to the market-place tomorrow and you shall have your money.' Now that the deal was made the Sheriff relaxed and poured himself more wine.

'That is not possible,' Robin said, 'for they are grazing here, there and everywhere, all over my scattered lands, and I could not get them together in time. But if you would like to come with me and see for yourself what fine beasts they are, and bring the money with you, we can seal our bargain on the spot.'

'Very well,' said the Sheriff, too eaten up with greed to consider whether he was wise to accept Robin's plan so readily, 'I will instruct my clerk to draw up a paper for the sale so that neither of us can go back on our word. What is your name, friend?'

'Robert Greenwood, sire.'

'Then, Robert Greenwood, as soon as we have finished our meal we will go together to find your herds.'

The feast did not end until late in the afternoon, and the Sheriff was not quite sober when he and Robin set off, Robin in his cart and the Sheriff on his horse. When they arrived at the edge of the forest the Sheriff, who had been boasting about his many successful business deals, suddenly fell silent and began to look about him nervously. Robin was whistling happily, planning his next move in the game he was playing, when the Sheriff gave a sharp exclamation.

'Stop that noise!' he said irritably. 'It is as well not to attract attention in these parts. Let us hope we do not meet a rogue called Robin Hood.'

'Robin Hood! Why, sire, I know him well, and I give you my word that you are in no more danger from him than you are from me!'

The Sheriff glanced at Robin sharply. 'That is little comfort. The fact that you are well acquainted with this outlaw is cause enough for alarm. I am beginning to wish I were well away from here.'

Robin tried to soothe his restless companion. 'Think of the cattle that will soon be yours, sire, and how little you are going to pay for them. Even if Robin Hood should appear on the scene, I promise you that he would do nothing that I would not do, and I am your friend, am I not?'

The Sheriff shrugged, and they rode on. At a bend in the path they came across a herd of red deer, grazing. The animals took fright at their approach and bolted.

Robin pointed after them. 'There you see some of my herd, master Sheriff. Are they not fat and fair?'

'But they are not cattle – they are the King's deer, surely?' The Sheriff was now definitely alarmed. 'You are no longer fair in my eyes, fellow. I do not care to continue with our business. You may keep your herds. I wish to leave the forest at once. You go your way, and I will go mine.'

Robin laughed, jumped down from the cart and took the Sheriff's bridle. 'Nay, my lord, you must not leave before meeting my brothers. You must dine with us as I did with you.' He raised his horn to his lips and blew three blasts. Almost before the notes had died away Little John was by his side, and a group of the outlaws, each carrying a yew bow.

'Welcome back, master,' Little John said, looking curiously at the agitated Sheriff.

'It is good to be back, Little John. I see you do not recognize our visitor. Men, let me present our worshipful master, the Sheriff of Nottingham, who has come to sup with us tonight. See that you greet him in a proper manner!'

The outlaws doffed their hats and bowed low to the Sheriff. Little John bent his knee in mock respect. 'Welcome to the greenwood, my lord!' he cried, and the men laughed and cheered. 'Welcome, Sheriff!'

'Greenwood!' The Sheriff darted a startled look at Robin Hood. 'That is what you said your name was – Robert Greenwood.'

'A slip of the tongue, sire,' said Robin, trying to keep a straight face. 'I should have said Robin Hood.'

The Sheriff shrank back. For once he could think of nothing to say. As they moved towards the heart of the forest his mind was in a turmoil. He cursed himself for having been taken in so easily. He wondered what was before him – certainly danger, perhaps even death. He wished with all his heart that he had never tried to play a trick on the young butcher. He clutched his saddle until his knuckles were white, and he had to clamp his teeth together to stop them from chattering.

At last they arrived at the forest clearing, and the Sheriff was allowed to dismount. He looked about him fearfully, half expecting to see a rope hanging from a tree, waiting for his neck to be put in the noose, and he was even more confused when Robin courteously invited him to sit next to him under the largest oak tree and began to talk about ordinary things – the weather, his health and that of his wife and family, the number of archers he kept, the price of wine …

Gradually the Sheriff began to regain his composure. Surely, he thought, these men could not be planning to kill him after treating him so politely. The feeling grew stronger as a great feast was being prepared and savoury, mouth-watering smells filled his nostrils. Then, before they were ready to eat, there was entertainment – quarter-staff contests, wrestling, the best archers displaying their skill. At the feast there was roast venison, capons, pasties, all washed down with sack, Malmsey wine and ale.

And when the sun had gone down and only a pale

moon and the last flickers of the dying fires lit the clearing, the Sheriff rose unsteadily to his feet. His head was swimming and his speech was slurred, but he insisted on speaking.

'I thank you, good yeomen all,' he said, swaying slightly, 'and Robin Hood too, one-time butcher, for the hos-hospitality you have given me this night. I am grat-grati-gratified that you have shown such respect for King Richard, through me, his deputy in Nottingham. I hope we may meet again sometime—'

'We will,' Robin muttered under his breath.

'But the sh-shadows have grown long, and I have far to go. I will be much in your debt if you will show me the road that I must take to get back to Nottingham.'

Robin got up. 'If it is your will to go, sire, then go you must.' The Sheriff began to move towards his horse, but a sudden sharpness in Robin's voice brought him to a halt. 'There is one thing you have forgotten.'

'Forgotten? Surely I have thanked you enough?' A hint of trouble to come pierced the fog of the Sheriff's mind, and he tittered nervously.

'Indeed you have, but here in the greenwood it is the custom for a guest to pay for his meal,' and Robin barred his way.

The Sheriff licked his lips. 'It had slipped my mind. I am sorry. We have all had a merry time, and even if you had not asked I would have offered you some payment. Would twenty pounds be a suitable sum?'

'It would not!' said Robin. 'I would be full of shame if we had not provided more than twenty pounds' worth of entertainment for you. Three hundred pounds, sire, is a more fitting sum for one of your eminence.'

The Sheriff, sober in an instant, exploded. 'Three hundred pounds! The devil take you, rogue! Your miserable feast and your shoddy games were hardly worth three pounds, let alone three hundred!'

'Sheriff, do not speak so angrily, I pray you. Though I love you for the feast you gave me in Nottingham this day, there are others here who do not love you at all, no, not at all. Is that not so, men?'

Not one of the men spoke, but slowly they formed a ring round the frightened Sheriff, and some drew their swords, others a stout cudgel, and a few began to fit arrows to their bows. The Sheriff knew when he was defeated, when neither bluff, bluster nor pleading was any use. He took out his purse and flung it at Robin's feet.

'Little John,' Robin said, 'take the reckoning. There will be three hundred pounds in that purse – the sum that this rascally man was going to pay me for beasts that were worth double. Only, unfortunately for him, those beasts did not exist ...'

Little John returned the empty purse to its owner, and Robin's stern attitude relaxed. 'Now, sire, our score is settled. Would you like one of us to lead you to your road?'

'I do not want any more of your hospitality,' the Sheriff said through clenched teeth. 'I will find my own way.'

'I cannot allow that,' said Robin, 'it would not be polite. Come, I will put you on the right road myself. It is the least a host can do.'

Taking the bridle rein of the Sheriff's horse, Robin led him to the broad path that met the main road. Then he smacked the horse's rump and the animal began to canter.

'Farewell, sire,' Robin called. 'I wish you many happy memories of this day. You are always welcome in Sherwood ...'

The Sheriff galloped back to Nottingham, poor in purse, foul of temper, but rich in experience. Robin returned to his men, well satisfied with his day's adventure.

Little John and the Sheriff

October had come to Sherwood Forest. Trees still bore leaves of gold and red, but many had begun to turn brown, and the ground was beginning to be covered by its autumn carpet. Mornings were chill and the sun, though bright, had lost its summer warmth. In the countryside the harvest had been gathered in, hops were plucked, and apples and pears lay ripe on attic floors. People everywhere were thinking of the coming winter, and making preparations against the cold days and long nights ahead. Wine and beer were stored in barrels, meat was salted and hung from the rafters, and fish was pickled in brine.

One event remained, however, to provide entertainment and merriment for the people of Nottingham and the surrounding villages before winter darkness kept them round the fireside, and that was the Goose Fair, held every year for three weeks on a large green space just outside the main gate leading into the town. Rows of booths made little streets, there were canvas tents decorated with streamers and flowers, and the alleys between them were crowded with men, women and children looking for sport and excitement. There was country dancing to enjoy, sweet cakes and barley sugar to buy, minstrels to listen to, and wrestlers, quarterstaff fighters and archers to watch. A lot of business was done too. Farmers came from far and near to sell and buy animals and birds, and geese especially were brought from Lincolnshire and Norfolk. Goose Fair was a time to remember and talk about for months.

Archery was the main sport, for the yeomen of Nottingham had the best reputation with the longbow in all the country. Usually the Sheriff of Nottingham offered money or a tun of ale as a prize for the best archer, but this year he put up two fat steers. He had not forgotten his adventure in Sherwood Forest and had not forgiven Robin Hood for the way he had been tricked and forced to part with three hundred pounds. He thought that the outlaws would not bother to compete for a prize that only cowherds would be interested in, and hoped that they would keep away from the town on the day of the contest.

When Robin Hood heard what the archery prize was to be he was angry. He guessed that the Sheriff's motive was to persuade the outlaws not to compete in an event they were likely to win, and he was half-inclined to let the Sheriff have his way.

But Little John had other ideas. 'I know that two steers, however fat they be, mean little to us when we can take our fill of the tenderest venison,' he said, 'but, master, we must not let the wily Sheriff think that he will see nothing of us. I would not like him to rest easy in his bed that night. Cannot I go and take part in the contest?'

Robin laughed at his friend's eagerness. 'You are a stout fellow,' he said, clapping Little John on the shoulder, 'but you lack the cunning that Will Stutely and I have, so if you do go, you must wear some disguise so that you will not be recognized and clapped into prison. You know that there is a price on your head, as there is on mine.'

'I will be careful,' Little John promised. 'I will wear a suit of scarlet instead of this green, and I will keep the cowl of my jacket drawn over my head the whole time, so that my hair and beard are not seen. In fact, I might even cut off my beard—'

'Nay, you must not do that,' Robin protested. 'We know what store you set on all that hair on your face, and it might not grow again!' Then he became serious. 'Take great care, my friend. You are my right-hand man, and I cannot do without you.'

Little John nodded and his huge hand clasped his master's thin brown one. 'I will be careful,' he said, 'but we must not let the Sheriff think we are afraid of him.'

The next day Little John, in a disguise that changed everything about him except his height, set out for Nottingham. He arrived at the fair and stood for a while watching the jostling throng, hearing the shouts and laughter, and soon began to feel the need for action. He drank some ale at one of the booths, then went to another where there was dancing. He joined in, leaping so high and capering so wildly, that many a young woman swore she had never seen such an energetic fellow in all her life.

Then a horn announced that the archery contest was about to begin, and Little John made his way to the butts. The Sheriff, with his nobles about him, sat on a dais near the target. He had searched the crowds anxiously with his eyes, and had given a sigh of relief when he had seen no one who resembled one of the hated outlaws. Even when the tall, scarlet-clad figure with his face hidden by a hood stepped forward with the other contestants, his suspicions were not aroused.

There were twelve bowmen in the line, among them some of the best in the counties of Lincolnshire and Nottinghamshire. The one in red stood inches taller than the rest. The shooting began, and eleven of the archers shot well, most of them reaching the target with two of their three shots. Last of all came the stranger's turn, but instead of fitting his arrow to his bow he turned to the dais and bowed. 'By your leave,' he said to the Sheriff, 'I would like to shoot at a mark of my own placing.' He strode down the course with a slender peeled willow sapling, which he stuck upright in the ground a hundred yards behind the official target. He returned to his place. 'There is a man's mark,' he said challengingly. 'Will any man try it?'

A forester stepped forward and, without speaking, made careful preparations to shoot. The crowd had fallen silent, and the Sheriff and his friends were leaning forward, wondering what was about to happen. The man took a long and steady aim, and shot. But the arrow whistled by the mark and buried itself in the ground a few yards behind. There was a scornful laugh from the onlookers, and the man turned away to hide his annoyance.

Then Little John, with hardly a glance at the target, lightly loosed his arrow. It flew unerringly through the air and split the willow wand straight down the middle. There was a ringing cheer from the crowd, and hats were flung into the air.

'Long live the red archer!' they cried. 'Hurray for the tall stranger!'

The Sheriff stepped down from the platform and came to where the archers stood. All but Little John doffed their caps, but he remained silent and still.

The Sheriff looked keenly at him. 'You are the best archer I have ever seen,' he said. 'What is your name and where were you born?'

'I was born in Yorkshire,' Little John replied, 'and men call me Reynold Greenleaf. I go about from place to place, seeking to improve my fortune.'

'Have I not seen you before?' said the Sheriff. 'There is something familiar about you.'

'You may have done,' Little John replied, shrugging his shoulders, 'for I have often seen you, sire.'

The Sheriff dismissed his vague feeling. 'You are a sturdy fellow,' he went on, 'and I could do with someone like you in my service. Will you join my household? You will receive good wages and plenty to eat and drink.'

Little John was not expecting such an offer, and he hesitated before speaking. His first thought was to refuse. He had no wish to be in close contact with the Sheriff, for the man was proud and mean and neglected the poor people of Nottingham. He saw no advantage in leaving his carefree life in the forest for one in the stifling atmosphere of a castle, surrounded by people he did not like or trust. But, he thought, there might be a chance of serving Robin Hood by getting into the enemy's camp. How, he did not yet know, but if it were possible, then he must not miss that chance.

So, smiling slightly, he agreed. 'Good wages and a full stomach?' he said. 'Right gladly will I enter your service, sire, and I trust I shall serve my master well.' My master, Robin Hood, he added to himself.

'Good,' said the Sheriff, delighted at engaging such a skilled marksman. Perhaps, he thought, I shall be able to use him against Robin Hood! 'Take your prize, and I will add a tun of brown ale for good measure. I shall now return to the castle. Follow me shortly.'

'I will come now,' said Little John, 'for I shall give

the steers and ale to all these good people, so that they may remember the red archer and know that he is their friend.'

To the cheers of the onlookers, excited at the thought of free meat and free ale, Little John followed the Sheriff's procession to the grim grey castle that stood on the hill at the edge of the town.

Little John found life easy in the Sheriff's service. He had little work to do and slept late in the mornings. He enjoyed hunting and hawking. He ate rich dishes and drank good beer, so that after six months he had grown fat and lazy, and the memory of life in the greenwood was blurred and distant. At first he had tried to think of ways by which his presence in the castle might be used to the advantage of the outlaws, but now his mind was a blank. His manliness had been eaten away by soft living.

It was good for Little John that this state of affairs was not to last. One fine spring morning, with the sun shining in at his window and the scent of woodbine filling the air, he lay in bed, wondering vaguely what to do with himself when he did get up, for he knew that the Sheriff and several companions had gone hunting without him. Suddenly, from far away, he heard the thin, faint sound of a horn, almost like the familiar note that Robin Hood blew, and in an instant the memory of all he was missing with his friends in the forest flooded into his mind, and he knew that he must get back to the life he knew and loved best.

'I have been a fool all these months,' he muttered. 'What will Robin and the others be thinking of me?

43

How could I have stayed in this place so long? I will go back to the forest today – now!' He leapt out of bed and bundled on his clothes.

When he got downstairs he saw the Sheriff's steward standing by the pantry door, jangling the keys that hung from his girdle. Although the steward was immensely fat, he was far from jolly and nobody liked him. When he saw Little John he grinned in an unpleasant way. 'What do you want with me this time of the morning?' he asked.

Little John put on an appealing expression. 'Master steward, I am a hungry man, not used to fasting. Will you give me something to eat from your pantry for I have a long journey ahead of me?'

'Sir Lie-a-bed, it is too late in the day to be talking of eating. You must wait till my lord comes back. Meanwhile, you had better take your appetite back to bed and put off your journey till tomorrow.'

At this Little John lost his temper. 'You great barrel of fat!' he shouted, raising one of his huge fists. 'Food I want, and you shall not stop me. If you will not open the pantry door, I will break it down!' He gave a great blow to the stout wooden door with his fist and one of the panels cracked. Another blow shattered another panel, and a third made such a gaping hole in the door that he was able to stoop and reach through the opening to where a venison pasty and a cold roast pheasant lay on the nearest shelf.

But the steward was not going to give in so easily. He quickly unfastened the bundle of thick iron keys from his girdle and brought them down on Little John's head with such force that his ears rang and stars danced before his eyes.

He span round dizzily, pushing the steward in the chest. The man overbalanced, fell and bumped his head on the stone floor and lay as though dead. But his groans

showed that he was still alive, and soon he was making an effort to get up.

Little John put one foot on the steward's chest and he sank back. 'Stay there,' Little John said, 'till you find the strength to go to bed. And never again keep a hungry man from his breakfast.' He rescued the pasty and the pheasant, found a flask of wine, sat down at a table and prepared to make a hearty meal.

In the kitchen across the courtyard the chief cook had heard the raised voices and came running across the court and up the steps to the pantry. He saw Little John at the table and the steward still on the floor. 'What is going on?' he demanded.

'Our master's favourite ne'er-do-well has knocked me down,' the steward whimpered, 'and is now stealing the food put out for my lord's supper. Not only is he a bully, he is also a thief. I would not like to be in his shoes when my lord returns.'

'Pah,' said Little John. 'My shoes would be too big for him anyway.'

'Is this true?' asked the cook.

Little John gulped and finished a mouthful of venison. 'You have eyes in your head,' he said curtly.

'You are an impudent fellow,' said the cook, who was always ready to speak his mind. 'Big as you are, I have a mind to give you a thrashing you will never forget.'

Little John put back his head and roared with laughter. 'Come then, have a go! Draw your sword, and I will draw mine, and when you are stretched out on the floor like that bladder of lard I will continue my breakfast.'

He got up from the table leisurely and advanced to

the cook, who was dancing with rage, his sword quivering in his hand. He drew his own sword and they crossed weapons.

Backwards and forwards they stamped, and the sound of the clashing swords was like the din of a blacksmith's shop. But, try as they might, neither could strike the other enough to draw blood, and each was able to parry the other's blow so that it failed to reach its target. For almost an hour they struggled, and the fight might have gone on for ever without result if Little John had not suddenly cried out, 'Hold, good cook! You are not going to carve me up, nor I you, that is certain. There is no point in going on till midnight and into tomorrow! Let us cry enough.'

The cook dropped his sword willingly. His face was purple and he could scarcely speak, but he managed to gasp out, 'You are right – I shall never make mincemeat of you—'

By this time the steward had rolled to his feet and wobbled off to bed, taking his aching head with him, fearful that he might get involved in the fight. Little John and the cook leaned against the wall, and gradually got their breath back. 'What were we fighting for?' said Little John. 'I did not know you were friendly with that fat steward.'

The cook scratched his head. 'I am not,' he said. 'I bear no love for him at all. I cannot think *why* we were fighting. Perhaps it was because I get so little chance to use my sword!'

'I know where you could practise to your heart's content.' Little John gave his companion a sly look.

'And where is that?'

'In Sherwood Forest.'

The cook looked at Little John in amazement. 'But that is where Robin Hood lives with his outlaws!'

'That is the place.'

'Then – then – do you mean to say you are one of them?' The cook moved a couple of paces away from the big man who was grinning at his goggling eyes.

'I am indeed. I am Little John, Robin Hood's right-hand man. What do you say to living in the greenwood with us? You are certainly the best swordsman I have ever clapped eyes on, and you would be a very useful member of our band.'

The cook shook his head as though he could not believe his ears. 'To think of it – Robin Hood's man here – in Nottingham Castle – in the service of the Sheriff! And none of us suspected you!' He tugged at his lower lip, thinking hard. 'Do you know, I have half a mind to do as you suggest. I have long wanted a change from town life, and from what I have heard I think the life of an outlaw would suit me well.' He paused, then said firmly, 'I will come with you.'

Little John was delighted. 'We will waste no more time then, but be on our way.' He began to lead the way through the courtyard, but suddenly stopped. 'I have been away from my master for six long months. It would be fitting that I should take him a present …' He turned back into the castle, and the mystified cook drummed his heels and looked nervously about him, hoping that the Sheriff would not return from hunting before his usual time. Presently Little John returned, a full sack over his shoulder, and a broad grin on his face.

'What have you got there?' asked the cook.

'An odd trifle or two,' Little John answered carelessly. 'A silver vessel, some silver plate, spoons, flagons – nothing much …'

The cook gulped. 'We had better go quickly. I would not like to see my lord's face when he finds out what has happened.'

The two men crossed the courtyard, swung out of the gate and into the town, where they avoided the busy streets and made their way from one alley to another until they were out in the open countryside. At every step they took towards the friendly shelter of the great forest, Little John's heart grew lighter.

They came upon Robin Hood and several of the men sprawling at their ease on the grass in the clearing. Robin sprang to his feet, his face alight with pleasure. 'Welcome!' he cried. 'It is so long since we have seen you, I had begun to think you had forgotten your friends. How have you been faring?'

Little John shook his hand warmly. 'I have been living in great style at the Lord Sheriff's,' he said, 'and I have come straight from the castle today. See, I have brought you his cook who, though you may not believe it, is as good a swordsman as I am.'

'Your name, friend?' Robin said politely.

'Much,' said the cook.

'Much what?' Robin turned a puzzled eye to Little John.

'My name is *Much*. My father was a miller in Mansfield, and I am generally known as Much the miller's son. A mouthful of words, but it saves me from having to listen to bad jokes!'

'Welcome, Much the miller's son,' Robin said quickly. 'Now, Little John, what have you to tell us?'

Little John told them all that had happened to him since he had gone to Goose Fair, not forgetting to admit how he had been led into soft living and lazy thinking. He described his encounter with the steward and his fight with the cook. Then he added, 'Before we left, the Sheriff insisted that I should bring you a gift ...' He upended his sack and a shower of silver articles poured on to the ground.

Robin looked grave. 'I am glad you have returned to us for we have missed you sorely. But, Little John, you should not have stolen the Sheriff's plate like a common thief. He had already been punished by us, to the tune of three hundred pounds.'

Little John saw the truth of Robin's remarks, but he was vexed at being scolded before his comrades, and decided to treat the whole thing lightly.

'If you do not think that the Sheriff did give us his treasures,' he said, 'I will fetch him here so that he can tell you himself. He is hunting somewhere in the forest today, and I think I know where he is likely to be at this moment. It is about five miles away. Do you give me permission to go?'

Robin gave a good-natured laugh. 'I have had to do without you for six months, so another hour or two will not hurt. But be sure you *do* come back!'

'That I will, master, and with the Sheriff!' Little John was soon lost to sight in the undergrowth.

He had to tramp through the dense forest for about two hours before he heard the sound of voices and came across the Sheriff and his friends preparing to finish their day's hunting. Remembering he was still supposed to be the Sheriff's man, he took off his cap and bent his knee. 'God save you, master,' he said.

'How now, Reynold Greenleaf,' said the surprised Sheriff. 'What are you doing here? I thought you would still be in bed!'

'I have been in the forest,' Little John answered, 'and I have seen such a sight that man's eyes have never beheld before. I saw a young hart all in green from top to toe, surrounded by a herd of about seventy deer, and they too were dressed in green. Their antlers were so sharp that I dared not shoot for fear the rest would turn on me and kill me.'

'That's a strange story,' said the Sheriff. 'Are you sure you have not been dreaming?'

'If you will come with me, good master,' Little John went on, 'I will show you this fair sight, and you may take them for your own herd. But you must come alone, lest the other men frighten them away. Come, sire, we shall not have far to go, and it really is a sight you should see.'

The Sheriff's greed overcame any doubts he might have about the likelihood of Little John's story. He told his companions to wait until he returned and turned his horse in the direction that Little John had already taken. Riding slowly so that his supposed servant could keep up with him he found himself being led down one twisting path after another until he was completely lost, in a part of the forest he had never been in before.

Finally they came into a great clearing, and the Sheriff saw a figure he recognized immediately sitting beneath the shade of an oak tree. 'See, master Sheriff,' said Little John, 'there is the hart I was telling you about. Is he not dressed all in green?'

The Sheriff exploded into a volcano of rage. 'Hart!' he spat out. 'That is Robin Hood, the scoundrel who tricked me once before.' Another thought struck him. 'And you – you must be Little John, as big a rascal as he is. What a blind fool I have been! I should have known ... Villain, you have betrayed me. I took you into my service and treated you well, and this is how you repay me.'

'You are right,' Little John laughed. 'I am indeed that villain. But let me tell you, this would not have happened if your steward had not refused me food when I asked for it. Still, as I sat at your table every day for six months, so you will now sit at ours.'

'Not again!' the Sheriff shuddered. 'I would as soon sit down with a nest of adders!'

Robin Hood was now by their side. 'Welcome, good Sheriff,' he said. 'Did I hear you say you have come to share another feast with us?'

The Sheriff glared at him. 'I am not hungry today.'

'That is a pity,' said Robin, 'for it would have been a good feast. We have a new cook – I daresay you have heard of Much the miller's son? He is longing to try his hand at a dish fit for a Sheriff. But if you will not eat, you must take a drink with us instead.' He beckoned to one of the outlaws, who brought forward a silver flagon on a silver plate.

The Sheriff stretched out his hand, then drew it back sharply. 'That cup – that plate – why, they are mine! Rogues – thieves – I will – you deserve – I promise you—' He spluttered into silence. He drew his black brows together, wondering bitterly what was going to happen to him next, what new trick these laughing outlaws were going to play on him. 'I shall be lucky if I escape with my life,' he thought.

He was entirely unprepared for what did happen. Robin Hood motioned him to get off his horse and led him to a seat next to his own under the oak. Then he spoke firmly, but kindly, so that the fears the Sheriff had for his safety gradually disappeared.

'Master Sheriff,' Robin Hood said, 'the last time you came to Sherwood Forest was to cheat a spendthrift young butcher, as you thought, and it turned out that you were cheated instead. But this time you have come for harmless pleasure and not to do anyone an injury. I take my tithes from fat priests and lordly squires, to help those who have been robbed and wronged. On this occasion you have wronged nobody, though no doubt in the future our paths will cross again and you will have to be taught a lesson. Because you have been generous to my good Little John for all these months you shall not go unrewarded. So you may take back your goods, and today I will not take a farthing from you. We will return your silver to the sack, and I myself will lead you back to your friends.'

The Sheriff scrambled to his feet, eager to be gone. His pride was hurt and he hated having to feel grateful to someone who had made him look foolish. He kept his eyes down as Robin Hood slung the sack over his shoulder and beckoned him to follow him out of the clearing.

They tramped through the forest in silence, the Sheriff leading his horse by the bridle rein. When they had got to within a few hundred yards from where the Sheriff had left his companions, Robin stopped and handed over the sack. 'I will leave you now,' he said, 'and here is a piece of advice to take with you. Make quite sure you know who you take into your service and do not be so ready to engage a complete stranger. Who knows, next time I might come knocking at your door! Oh, and tell your steward to mend his manners! Farewell. I am sorry you will have no chief cook to prepare your meal tonight!'

The Sheriff's answer was an ill-tempered grunt.

The hunters were amazed to see him come out of the forest bearing a sack on his shoulders, and though they questioned him closely he remained silent all the way back to the castle.

The wedding of Allan-a-Dale

It was early one summer morning. The dew still sparkled on the grass. The day gave promise of heat to come and Robin Hood, lying under his favourite tree, was feeling content. Will Stutely was lying at full length on one side of him, his hands clasped behind his head, and Little John sat on the other side, making a cudgel out of a crabapple tree limb. Others of the band were sitting or lying nearby.

They were listening to Will Scarlet, the best among them at telling stories. He was just finishing one of his best-loved tales, that of King Arthur and Guinevere

55

and their court at Camelot, and when he came to the end his listeners sighed with pleasure.

'It makes a man better to hear of the noble men and women of old,' said Will Stutely.

'I sometimes wish we lived in those brave times,' said Little John.

'At least they did not wonder where the next meal was coming from,' said the practical Robin. 'Do you realize that we have had nobody to dine with us for weeks? After paying for the cloth we need to make us all new clothes our money will be almost gone. We must replenish our store quickly. Will Stutely, enough of noble men and women. Choose a few men and go to the Fosse Way to see if you can find a traveller to eat with us this evening. The richer and more rascally he is, the better!'

Will sprang to his feet willingly. 'I'm glad you have chosen me,' he said. 'My limbs are getting slack from idleness. Will Scarlet, I'd like you with me, and—' he pointed to three more outlaws – 'you and you and you. We'll do our best to find a big belly and a fat purse to bring back, master.'

The five men set out for the Fosse Way that ran arrow-straight through Newark to Lincoln. All day they stayed near the highway, hidden behind a hawthorn bush, eating cold meats and drinking beer. Many people passed as they waited, but not one traveller was suitable to be a guest of Robin Hood. They saw neither abbot, squire nor merchant.

The sun began to sink low. The sky grew red and shadows lengthened. Birds twittered sleepily, and from a distance they heard a milkmaid calling her cows home to be milked.

Will Stutely got to his feet. 'What bad luck we have had – not a bird worth shooting has come within reach. Come, lads, we had better tell Robin that there will be no guest tonight.'

His companions gathered up their belongings and they began to trudge dejectedly through the forest. They had not gone far, however, when Will Stutely, whose ears were as sharp as those of a fox, suddenly stopped in his tracks. He motioned to the others. 'Ssh! I can hear something.'

They all listened intently, then gazed at each other in bewilderment, for the sound that came to their ears was a lamentation, a low, melancholy wail.

'We must look into this,' said Will Scarlet, always quick to help anybody in distress.

'Careful,' Will Stutely warned him. 'Robin Hood never seems to mind thrusting his finger into a boiling pot, but I see no sense in meeting trouble if it can be avoided. It is a man's voice, without a doubt, and a man should be able to deal with his own difficulties.'

'Do not talk like that,' Will Scarlet protested. 'Stay here if you like, but I'm going to see what is the matter.'

Will Stutely was quick to change his mind. 'And have you all think that I am afraid? Not likely! Of course I will come with you.'

He crept forward, his companions following in single file, until they came to an opening in the woodland. There they saw, lying face downward beneath the branches of a willow tree, a youth, sobbing quietly. His fair hair was tangled, his clothes were awry. From one of the branches hung a harp of polished wood inlaid with gold and silver. Beside him lay a bow and a quiver spilling out its arrows. It was a pathetic sight, and the hearts of the outlaws were touched.

'Hallo there,' Will Stutely called. 'Who are you, and why are you killing the grass with salt water?'

The stranger raised a tearstained face. He leapt to his feet, snatching up his bow, and fitted an arrow to it, ready, in spite of his woe, to defend himself against these rough-looking men.

One of the outlaws peered at the youth and said quietly, 'I know that lad. He is a minstrel, and very popular in these parts. A while ago he was striding about with a flower at his ear and a cock's feather in his cap. What a change in him now!'

Will Stutely strode forward impatiently. 'Put up your bow, young fellow, we are not going to harm you. Wipe your eyes and stop snivelling like a girl whose pet starling has died.'

But Will Scarlet, milder of manner and quicker to sympathize, put Will Stutely aside, and laid his hand on the youth's shoulder. 'You are in trouble. Come with us, and we will take you to someone who might be able to help you. I will carry your harp for you. Come, pick up your arrows, there is not far to go.'

Sniffing, but a little more cheerful at the prospect of help, the youth did as he was told. With bowed head, he accompanied the outlaws, walking beside Will Scarlet.

Soon a faint red glow told them that they were near their destination. In the glade, now bathed in moonlight, they came across the rest of the outlaws. A great fire crackled, and roasting on it were steaks of venison, pheasants and fish from the river. The air was filled with good smells. Robin Hood, on his mossy seat, with Little John in attendance, looked up as Will Scarlet urged the young stranger forward.

'Good evening, fair friend,' said Robin. 'Have you come to dine with us?' This was no fat goose for the plucking, but he did not show his surprise.

'Alas, I do not know,' said the youth, looking about him in a dazed way. 'Truly, I do not know whether I am awake or dreaming.'

'You are awake right enough,' said Robin, laughing. 'You are not who I expected to see, but you are welcome nevertheless. You will be our honoured guest tonight.'

The youth shook his head as though to rid himself of his confused thoughts. He looked around him, then more closely at the man who was obviously the leader of the group. He began to stammer with a mixture of excitement and fear. 'I know now who you are – you must be – you are – are you Robin Hood – the great Robin Hood?'

'You have hit the bull's eye!' Robin said. 'Now you know who I am, you also know that whoever feasts with me must pay for their meal. I hope you have a full purse with you.'

'Alas,' said the youth, 'I have no money at all – except half a silver coin, the other half of which my dear love carries, hung round her neck on a silken thread.'

A great shout of laughter went up from the outlaws, and the youth looked ready to die with shame. But Will Scarlet explained how they had come across the weeping boy and how he thought Robin might be able to help him, whatever his trouble was. 'He is not the kind of guest you were expecting, but he is the only one we could find!'

Robin looked closely at the boy's pale face and brimming eyes. 'Grief can come to the young as well as the old,' he said. 'Tell me your name.'

'It is Allan-a-Dale.'

'I have heard of you,' Robin said. 'You are a minstrel whose voice charms all who hear it. How old are you?'

'Nineteen,' the youth replied.

'Too young to have so many cares on your shoulders,' Robin said. 'Come, sit down beside me and tell me your story. Stay with us, Will Scarlet and Little John. The rest of you can get on with preparations for dinner.'

Allan-a-Dale's story did not take long. He told his listeners how, on his travels, he had stopped at a farmhouse and had played and sung to the farmer's family. The eldest daughter, named Alice, as lovely as the first snowdrop in spring, had fallen in love with him, and he with her. But as she knew her father would never agree to her marrying a poor minstrel, they had had to meet secretly, and by the banks of the River Maun they had broken a sixpence between them as a token of their love and had vowed to be true to each other for ever.

It was not long before the farmer discovered what had

been going on. Furious, he had sent Alice away from home to live with relatives in another part of the country, and since then Allan-a-Dale had been wandering from place to place, singing his sad songs, playing his melancholy tunes and always searching, but in vain, for his lost love.

'This morning,' he said, 'I heard that she has come home to be married to a rich man old enough to be her grandfather. She does not know him, she cannot love him, but it is her father's wish. That is why my heart is broken …'

'When is this wedding to take place?' Robin asked thoughtfully.

'Why, sir, tomorrow, at Woodhouse Church, at three o'clock, and the Bishop of Hereford is to perform the ceremony. Alas, I shall never see my dear Alice again.' The young man's eyes filled with tears.

'No more tears, I pray you!' exclaimed Robin. 'I have a plan that will deliver the maiden up to you. Are you willing to do what I say?'

'If you will give me back my love,' Allan-a-Dale cried eagerly, 'I swear on the Holy Book that I will be your true servant for ever!'

'Good lad. We need a minstrel to keep us amused, and when you and Alice are married you must visit us often. Tomorrow we will go to Woodhouse, it lies scarce five miles from here as the crow flies. Will Stutely, you will arrange for twenty-four of our best men to be outside the church. Will Scarlet, you will deck out this young fellow with clothes fit for a wedding, and Much, I know you will be able to provide a sumptuous wedding feast. Tonight, Allan-a-Dale, you will taste the joys of sleeping in the open air. Tomorrow will be your wedding day!'

The next day the journey to Woodhouse seemed to take no time at all, so quickly did they travel, with Allan-a-Dale leading the way, almost as fleet as a deer. When they arrived at the church the guests were beginning to assemble. The Bishop was in the vestry, putting on his robes. He gave a start when he saw a green-clad minstrel stride boldly up to the church door and peer inside. It was Robin Hood, who had borrowed Allan-a-Dale's harp.

The Bishop hurried down the aisle to the door. 'Who are you, fellow?' he rapped out. 'What are you doing here? I did not know that a minstrel had been invited to the wedding.'

Robin bowed low. 'May it please your reverence,' he said humbly, 'I am only a strolling minstrel, but men say I play the harp better than anyone else in the north country, and I hoped that I might add to the happiness of the bride and groom this afternoon.'

'What tunes can you play?' the Bishop demanded.

'I have one so merry that a lover will forget he has been jilted,' Robin said, 'and another that will make a bride forsake her groom at the altar. I can play a tune that will bring two loving souls together even though they may be five miles apart.'

'Very well,' said the Bishop, 'you may stay and grace our ceremony. I like the harp well. Stand to one side now, for here comes the wedding party.'

Up the lane to the church hobbled an old man, with

ten archers in scarlet and gold walking slowly before him. After them came a pretty girl, leaning on her father's arm. Her face was pale and tearstained, and her body drooped like a lily with a snapped stem. Two maids of honour followed her, one to hold up her white dress, the other carrying flowers.

The procession reached the door, where Robin was still standing. He spoke so loudly that everybody heard him. 'Why, this is surely the worst matched pair that ever entered a church to be wed!' He let the archers and the hunched old bridegroom go past then hurried to the maiden and whispered to her, 'Courage, lass. There is another minstrel nearby who may play more to your liking. You will see him soon.'

'Stand aside, fellow!' cried Alice's father. 'I do not know who you are, but you will leave my daughter alone.'

'Nay, I have but come to bring her good luck,' said Robin. He followed the pair into the church and up to the chancel where the Bishop stood waiting.

'Let us have a tune before the ceremony begins,' the Bishop said. 'Strike up your harp, fellow, to make us all merry.'

'I will gladly do as you say,' Robin replied, 'if you will let me choose another instrument. I think the horn makes the merriest music in all the world.' He drew his horn from beneath his green cloak, and blew three notes that made the church rafters ring.

There was an amazed silence in the church, then a hubbub of noise. 'Seize him!' the Bishop roared. 'There is mischief afoot! Something tells me that Robin Hood is behind all this!'

The ten liveried archers rushed forward from their places, but before they could reach Robin there was another commotion at the door, and twenty-four sturdy bowmen marched in, with Will Stutely at their head and Little John bringing up the rear. They seized the archers, the bride's scowling father and the bemused old man, two outlaws to each man. Then in came Allan-a-Dale, decked out in fine clothes, and with him Will Scarlet. They walked down the aisle and stopped at the chancel. The Bishop, his eyes starting from his head, could find no words.

Robin took Alice's hand. 'Before a young girl weds she chooses who she wants to marry,' he said. 'Now, my dear, before this wedding continues, who will you have for a husband?'

Alice did not answer in words, but smiled, walked over to Allan-a-Dale, and flung her arms around his neck. They both burst into tears. The maids of honour began to giggle.

'She has chosen well,' Robin declared. 'Now, my Lord Bishop, proceed with the ceremony.'

'You trickster!' the Bishop shouted. 'I will not marry them, for the law says that banns must be called three times in the church before a marriage can take place. The banns have been called for the knight you have so disgracefully treated, not for this popinjay here. You have overstepped the mark this time, outlaw.' He shut his book up with a snap and tucked it under his arm.

Robin turned from him impatiently. 'Come here, Little John,' he called. 'Take my Lord Bishop's robe

and put it on yourself. What manner of bishop will you make, I wonder?'

Seeing the size of the outlaw who towered over him, the Bishop offered no resistance, and Little John was soon dressed as a priest. The gown hung loosely from his shoulders and came only to his knees. It was a comical sight, and people began to laugh. Alice's attendants became almost hysterical.

'Hush, good people,' Robin said. 'You see before you the finest bishop in the land. Little John, call the banns.'

Little John clambered awkwardly into the pulpit, his gown fluttering around him, and with great dignity he called the banns for the marriage of Allan-a-Dale and Alice three times, according to the law. He made to get down, but Robin stopped him.

'That is not enough. Your gown is so short you must talk longer.'

The banns were called three more times in Little John's ringing tones, and when he had finished a cheer went up from the outlaws. 'You ought to get a treble fee for that!' one of them called out.

'Now we will have the wedding,' Robin said. He pulled the Bishop forward. 'Everything has been done as the law demands. The maiden has chosen her man, and the man his maid. Bishop, marry them!'

The Bishop gave in with as good a grace as he could muster, and mumbled through the marriage service. While he was doing it the old man looked as though he did not realize what was happening, shaking his head helplessly. Alice's father, straining against the arms of a couple of outlaws, gritted his teeth and muttered threats of vengeance. The maids of honour, envious of Alice's good fortune, were casting longing glances at the handsomest men present, and the rest of the congregation had decided to enjoy the proceedings as there was nothing they could do to alter things.

When the Bishop said surlily, 'Who giveth this maid?' Robin responded with a clear voice, 'I do – Robin Hood of Sherwood. And if anyone should try to take her away from Allan-a-Dale he shall pay dearly for his efforts!' He looked at Alice's father as he spoke, and the farmer subsided, knowing that he was beaten.

Almost dizzy with happiness, Alice and Allan-a-Dale became man and wife, and the bride was kissed by every outlaw present, beginning with Robin Hood.

Friar Tuck
joins the band

When the weather was fine and there was no urgent business on hand the outlaws spent a lot of time in sporting contests, partly for enjoyment, but also in order to keep themselves fit and ready to face the dangers that often threatened them. Their games frequently ended in a heated argument about who was the strongest, the swiftest or the bravest. Robin Hood heard Will Scarlet, Much the miller's son and Little John discussing, in raised voices, which of them could kill a hart, buck or doe from a distance of five hundred yards.

'Why bother to argue,' he said, 'on such a matter?

On his day each of you is the best. If I rode a hundred miles I could not find anyone to match you three.'

'Not so, master,' said Will Scarlet, shaking his head. 'I used to know someone who could beat us all at whatever we tried – and you too!'

Robin pricked up his ears. This was difficult to believe! 'And who may this excellent fellow be?' he asked.

'He was a friar of Fountains Abbey, but he has now left the order and is living a solitary life as a hermit. He is as much soldier as priest. He is nicknamed Tuck because as often as not his habit is tucked up around his waist so that he may have the freedom to wield a quarter-staff or a broadsword. Friar Tuck is quite a character in Fountain Dale.'

'Then,' Robin declared, 'I will neither eat nor drink until I have seen this friar and can prove your words to be true or false.'

'I will guide you there myself,' said Will, 'for I knew that part of the country well in the old days. We can get there and back in a day.'

'We will take with us Little John, David of Doncaster and Arthur-a-Bland,' said Robin. 'I will leave Will Stutely in charge, and Much, you see that there is plenty to eat when we return. Now I will dress myself for the enterprise.'

He put on a steel coat of chainmail, then his light jacket of Lincoln green. On his head he placed a steel cap and covered it with his usual one of soft green leather. He fastened a broadsword to his side, picked up his bow and arrows, and the five men set out.

Will Scarlet led them for some three hours through the forest until they came to a broad pastureland, through which ran a stream, dipping in and out through the willows and rushes on its banks. They walked for a long time by its side until Will suddenly stopped. The others were glad to stop too, for they were getting weary.

'Just beyond the next bend is a ford which is not deeper than mid-thigh in any place,' said Will, 'so you will have no difficulty in crossing. Somewhere on the other side is a cell built into a high bank amid the thickets, and there Friar Tuck lives. Shall we come further with you?'

'No,' said Robin, 'I would like to enjoy this adventure alone. All I ask is that if you hear me sound my horn, come quickly!'

Although Little John did not like being left behind if there was any chance of a fight, he agreed to stay with the others, with only a little grumbling.

Robin soon disappeared round the bend in the river. He stood on the bank, trying to make up his mind to let himself into the water and wade across. 'I wish I had not worn my armour,' he thought. 'I hope the water will not rust it. I shall have to get my feet wet, but that cannot be helped.'

While he was deciding to take the plunge he heard snatches of a song coming from the other side. Then came the sound of two men arguing about whether meat pie was better than game pie, especially when it was flavoured with young onions ...

'The friar must have a visitor,' Robin muttered. He listened again, and a puzzled look appeared on his face.

'Never have I heard two men talk more alike than those fellows yonder. They might well be twins. I will look into this matter.'

He crept quietly through the trees which overhung the river bank and peered across to the other side, making sure that he himself could not be seen. Sitting at his ease on the opposite bank, his back against a tree, half hidden by the ferns around him, was one of the fattest men Robin had ever seen. His head was as round as an apple and, except for the shaven crown, covered with a mat of close-cropped hair. He had a curly black beard, a neck as thick as a bull's, broad shoulders and limbs like young oak trees. His loose robe, tied in the middle with a cord, and a string of beads round his neck, showed that he was a friar, but a sword and buckler at his waist was as stout as Robin's own. A huge pie rested on each knee, and the friar evidently could not make up his mind which to eat first. He was talking to each in turn.

Finally, after taking a long pull from a flask of wine, he appeared to come to a decision. He thrust a hand into the meat pie and drew it out full of juicy lumps. Robin's mouth watered at the sight and he suddenly realized how hungry he was. Perhaps, he thought, there was a chance of getting his hands on the game pie – but first he had to cross the river.

He seized his bow and fitted an arrow. Then he called out, 'Hey, friar, I want to get to your side of the river, but I do not want to get my feet wet. So carry me over, will you? Do not refuse or I cannot answer for your safety.'

The friar started up at the unexpected greeting, and laid his hand on his sword. Then he saw that the arrow was pointing straight at his heart. 'Put your bow down, fellow,' he called back, 'and I will help you over. It is our duty in life to help each other, and I have good Saint Christopher as an example.'

He laid aside his pies, his sword and buckler, and began to wade across the stream. His eyes were twinkling with a cunning light, which Robin did not see, or he might have wondered why his order had been obeyed so readily.

When the friar had waddled close enough for Robin to clamber on his back he turned again and, in complete silence, took his burden to the opposite bank and deposited him on the grass.

'Thank you, good friar,' Robin said, looking at his dry feet in satisfaction, 'I am in your debt'.

'In my debt, are you?' said the friar, grabbing his sword. 'Then you shall repay that debt, and quickly. I have suddenly remembered that I have business on your side of the river, so I must ask that what I did for you, you do for me. *You* carry *me* across the water.'

Robin had been looking with covetous eyes at the game pie, but they suddenly swivelled to the glinting point of the friar's sword. He knew that he could neither unsling his bow from his back, where he had put it to avoid getting it wet, nor get to his scabbard for his sword in time to prevent an attack.

He tried to play for time. 'But, father, I shall get my feet wet, and that is what I particularly do not want to do.'

'Are your feet better than mine?' the friar retorted.
'My feet are already wet, and I fear that I shall get
rheumatism.' His sword twitched and Robin was sure
that he meant business.

He looked at the friar's girth and wondered what it
would be like with that mountain of flesh on his back.

'I am not as strong as you,' he complained. 'I would not like to fall and drop you in the water. Suppose you leave your sword and buckler behind to lighten my load, then I will carry you across.'

'Agreed,' said the friar without hesitation, and put down his weapon. Robin bent his back and the friar, with much grunting, heaved himself up.

The stones on the bed of the river were round and slippery, and in mid-stream the current was strong. Robin struggled on, almost bent double, lurching from one side to the other in a manner that threatened to unseat his rider and plunge them both beneath the water. The sweat poured off him, and he gasped like a winded horse. But at last he staggered on to the bank and rid himself of his unwieldy load.

Before the defenceless friar had time to set himself to rights Robin was standing over him, his own sword in his hand. Wiping the sweat from his brow he said, unable to keep a note of triumph from his voice, 'You thought you had turned the tables very neatly, did you not, friar? But what do the Scriptures say? Be not weary of well-doing ... Well, I am going to put you to the test. *You* will now carry *me* back again, or I will make cheese-cloth out of your habit!'

The friar looked at Robin, and again there was a cunning gleam in his eye, but his voice was as courteous as ever. 'You have keen wits, my son,' he said, 'and I can see that the water has not quenched your spirit. Once more I will bend my back to you. Mount your steed ... '

Robin took up his position again, his heels digging

into the friar's sides. He was feeling very pleased with himself, but his good humour vanished when they reached the middle of the river and he found himself heaved over the friar's head as though he were a sack of grain and deposited in the water with a mighty splash.

'There,' said the friar coolly. 'Let that make your spirit less haughty.'

Robin managed to struggle to an upright position, spat water from his mouth and shook it from his ears. The friar was already wading back to his own bank.

Robin shook his fist at the friar, whose shoulders were heaving with mirth. 'I am coming after you,' he roared, 'and I will turn you into minced meat before I have finished with you.' He started for the bank, slipping and sliding.

'Take your time,' the friar taunted him. 'I shall not run away.'

Robin reached dry land and began to roll up his sleeves. The friar tucked his robe higher round his waist and showed that he too was wearing a coat of chainmail. They both drew their swords at the same time.

'Look to yourself!' Robin cried.

'Nay, I must give that advice to you,' the friar replied grimly.

A fierce battle began. Right and left, up and down, back and forth they fought. The swords flashed in the sunlight, and then met with a clash that would have splintered less sturdy weapons. They were equally matched and each landed many a blow, but because they were both wearing chainmail they did each other no harm. While they were fighting each thought that never had he had such a worthy opponent, and wondered how the affair would end. But neither was inclined to give in.

Finally, in a furious onset of lunge and parry, Robin's foot slipped on a stone, and he went down on his knees. But the friar did not pursue his advantage. He waited for Robin to get to his feet again. 'I am ready for a rest if you are,' he said, his chest heaving.

'You are a generous fellow, as befits your cloth,' Robin said. 'You could have had me just then. Let us rest awhile before we begin again.'

They both flopped thankfully on to the grass, and for a few minutes neither spoke. When red faces had cooled down and they were able to speak without gasping, Robin said, though without much eagerness in his voice, 'I suppose it is time to start again?'

'I suppose so,' said the friar reluctantly.

'Before we do, I would like to ask a favour of you.'

'What is that?'

'I would like to blow three times on my horn.'

The friar drew his brows together. 'It is a trick, I have no doubt, but I will grant your request, providing you will grant mine.'

'And what is yours?'

'To put my hand to my mouth and whistle three times.'

'I have no objection if you want to practise being a blackbird,' said Robin. 'I will go first.' He raised his silver horn to his lips.

The three blasts echoed through the trees and over the fields. Hardly had Robin time to lower his horn than four tall men in Lincoln green came running to the river bank, each with a bow in his hand and an arrow quivering against the string. Three of them looked grim and determined, but though Will Scarlet held his bow as straight as the rest he seemed much more at ease.

'My men,' Robin said simply.

'I have some friends too,' said the friar, putting two fingers in his mouth and giving three piercing whistles.

There was a crackling among the bushes and from the covert burst four great shaggy hounds. 'A dog for every man of yours and I for you!' the friar cried. 'At 'em, boys!'

'This is not fair,' Robin began to protest, but he got no further before the dogs were upon him, showing their fangs and snarling. It was lucky for Robin that there was a tree nearby. He dropped his sword and leapt up to the lowest branch, twined his legs round it and swarmed up the trunk until he was safe.

The friar bellowed with laughter. 'Well done, friend! Now your men shall see how they like being dogs' meat.' He gave another command to the animals and pointed to the outlaws. 'Over the water and get 'em!'

When the outlaws saw the dogs making for the river they drew their arrows and let fly. But no arrow met its mark because each dog caught one in his mouth and bit it in two. They laid their trophies before the friar's feet as if they had been playing a game of fetching sticks. Once more four arrows whistled across the water, and again, and each time the dogs leapt lightly aside and retrieved the harmless weapons.

The outlaws dropped their bows, three of them muttering to themselves, wondering what to do should the dogs cross the river and attack them. 'I have never seen the like of this in all my born days,' Little John said.

'It is surely witchcraft,' David of Doncaster whispered.

Arthur-a-Bland turned pale. 'That friar must be the devil in disguise.'

Only Will Scarlet showed no fear. He stepped forward as the dogs began swimming across the river, and when they were clambering up the bank he met them without flinching. 'How now,' he said sternly to the leader. 'What is the meaning of this? Down, sir! Down, I say!'

The dog dropped to his haunches and looked up at the fearless outlaw. Then he crept forward, his tail beginning to wag, and licked Will's outstretched hand. The other dogs followed suit, and soon Will had four fawning animals trying to outdo each other in friendly advances. He turned a grinning face to his friends. 'Their bark is worse than their bite,' he said. 'I know these rascals from of old.'

Little John took a hesitant step forward and tickled one of the dog's ears. 'I am right glad we did not have to put that to the test,' he said. 'We had better get to the other side of the river and see what all this is about.'

'You can get down now, master,' Will Scarlet called to Robin. 'The danger is over.'

Men and dogs splashed through the water and joined Robin Hood and the friar. Robin was brushing himself down and trying not to feel foolish. Let anybody laugh at me, he thought fiercely, and he will feel my fist on his head.

But nobody was laughing. The friar was peering at Will Scarlet. 'What does this mean?' he said. 'Who is it that can turn wolves into lambs? The only fellow who could exact such obedience from these savage creatures is a youngster I knew long ago – his name was Will—'

'And still is!' Will cried gaily. 'Father, it is good to see you again.'

The friar seized Will's hand and pumped it up and down. 'Well met again, my boy. You have changed a great deal since I saw you last. I would hardly have known you, but the dogs, it seems, have better memories. What are you doing in this company of ruffians?'

'Not ruffians, father,' said Will. 'Outlaws, yes, but not ruffians. I can see that you do not know that I have joined Robin Hood's band.'

'Then this—' gasped the friar, 'this is Robin Hood. Why did you not tell me who you were?'

'Because you did not ask! I knew you were the Friar Tuck I was hoping to meet as soon as I saw your robe hitched up round your waist.'

The friar could not take his eyes off the grinning outlaw. 'I have been fighting the famous Robin Hood. Well, well …'

'And you beat me fairly,' said Robin. 'I always give credit where credit is due. I am glad that Will Scarlet knew your dogs. My heart nearly stopped when I saw those beasts coming towards me.'

'I never thought I would meet you in battle,' the friar went on. 'I can understand now why I had such a worthy opponent. Young Will is wise to have thrown in his lot with you. I have sometimes wished that I might join your band. Since leaving the order I have led a full life, but a lonely one.'

'Then why don't you join us, father?' said Will. 'May he, Robin?'

Robin rubbed his chin. 'We do need a good chaplain for the welfare of our souls, and, moreover, one who can fight when needs be. Friar Tuck, you are just the man for us!'

'I can cook too,' said Friar Tuck. 'To prove it, I will ask you to help me to finish off my pies, and over the wine perhaps you will tell me more about your doings. I hope you do not hold fast days – I could not go for a day without food.'

'We only fast when there is nothing to eat,' said Robin, 'and that is not very often, I assure you. Come now, where is that game pie? The only reason I wanted to cross the river was to get at it!'

Guy of Gisbourne

A sleek-headed blackbird, perched on a hawthorn bush, cocked his head sideways and peered at the two men walking side by side through the forest. Each man was wrapped in his own thoughts, and even the blackbird's loud chirping did not arouse them. When at last the silence was broken it was by both men speaking at once.

'Little John, I've been thinking—' said Robin Hood.

'Master, what do you say if—' said Little John.

They both laughed. 'Speak first,' said Robin.

'No, master, you speak first. I wonder if we have been having the same thoughts.'

'Well, this is what I have been thinking. Today is the first fine day after ten days of rain—'

'And it is time for an adventure!' Little John interrupted.

'That is just what I was going to say. Suppose each of us goes his own way—'

'Yes, we will make it a contest—'

'And when we meet at sundown,' Robin finished, 'we will tell the others what has happened to us and see which of us has had the most exciting time.'

'Capital,' agreed Little John. 'I have a feeling that both of us will have strange stories to tell.'

'We will part company where the path divides into two,' said Robin. 'I will take the left-hand path, and you the right. Good fortune, Little John.'

'Farewell, master, and a peaceful day to you!' said Little John.

Robin's day was to be very far from peaceful. He had not been walking for long before he felt a prickling in the back of his neck that told him he was not alone in the forest, that danger was very close. Cautiously he crept forward until he could see round the next curve in the path, then stopped dead in his tracks. For a moment he felt an unfamiliar twinge of fear.

Sitting in the shade of a tree was a creature that looked as though it were straight from the regions of the devil. It was a man, and yet surely it could not be a man, for from head to foot it was covered in a horse's hide. Upon its head was a cowl that hid its face, and which was also part of the horse's skin, the ears sticking up like those of a rabbit. The body was clad in a brown hairy jacket, the legs were similarly covered. But Robin had never seen a horse sitting down like a man, with a broadsword and a double-edged dagger by its side and a quiver of arrows hung across its shoulders. A bow of yew leaned against the tree.

No horse, then, but what kind of a man? Some half-witted fellow, surely, and nothing to fear. There might indeed be some fun to be got out of him, Robin thought, and he approached the weird figure.

'Hello, fellow,' he said, 'if fellow you be, for I have never seen such an odd sight in all my days. Who are you and why are you dressed like that?'

The man did not answer immediately, but pushed back his cowl and glowered at Robin, who was tempted to ask him to cover his face again, for it was as ugly and disagreeable as a face could be. The nose was thin and beak-like, the eyes were black and fierce, and the mouth looked like a slash of bad temper. The skin was sallow and deeply lined. He resembled a cruel bird of prey.

'Who are you?' Robin repeated. 'Or can you only neigh like the horse you pretend to be?'

'Never mind who I am,' the man growled in a voice like an ox-cart rolling over gravel. 'Who might you be, impertinent knave?'

'Now, fellow, have a care how you speak. I suspect you really are a horse that has fed on rough oats and vinegar, your voice is so sour.'

'If you do not like the way I speak, you had better go away quickly, for my deeds are even rougher than my voice.'

'Nonsense, friend,' said Robin, who was beginning to enjoy the encounter, 'I love the way you speak. You are so polite and witty that I could listen to you all day.'

The man looked at Robin as a dog looks at a man before he springs at his throat, and Robin wondered if he had not gone too far with his banter. But he returned the man's gaze with one of wide-eyed innocence, and for a minute there was a tense silence.

Then the man said coldly, 'It would be better for you if you were to tell me your name before I decide whether or not to kill you.'

Robin's laughter was not quite as natural as he would have liked. 'What a joker you are! My name may be this, or it may be that. It is of no importance, except to me. And as we have not met before it would be of no use to you. You are a stranger in this forest so it would be more polite for you to tell me your name and why you are dressed in such an outlandish way.'

'You are too bold, sire,' said the man. 'Why do I not kill you now and stop your prattling tongue? I slew a man only yesterday for saying much less than you have said. I will let you live a little longer, though, because you may be useful. I could say I wear these clothes to keep me warm. I could also say that this hide is as good as a coat of steel should anyone be foolish enough to thrust a sword at me.'

'A good reason,' said Robin, 'and it would not cost as much.'

'As for my name – it is Guy of Gisbourne. Are you any the wiser?'

Indeed I am, thought Robin. The notorious Guy of Gisbourne, thief and murderer; an outlaw too, but one who lived and worked on his own, hated by everyone who had come into contact with him. 'Yes, I have heard of you,' Robin said, 'you live in the woodlands of Herefordshire, do you not? I have heard of your gentle ways and kind deeds.'

Guy of Gisbourne gave an unpleasant laugh. 'That is one way of describing my activities! Now, who are you?'

'I am a King's Forester,' said Robin. 'I guard the King's deer against curious strangers.'

'Then you are the man I want, for I am here on the King's business.'

Robin was startled. 'What business can you do here for the King?'

'The Bishop of Hereford sent me to the Sheriff of Nottingham to do him a service, in return for which I am to get a free pardon and a fee of a hundred pounds.'

Robin was beginning to get an idea of what that service was. He felt anger rising inside him, but it did not show as he said, 'One hundred pounds? That is a lot of money.'

'I would kill my own brother for half of that,' said Guy of Gisbourne, 'but it is not my brother I have come here to seek. You have heard the saying, "Set a thief to catch a thief"?'

'And the thief you have come to catch?' Robin asked quietly.

'A certain outlaw called Robin Hood. Dead or alive, the Sheriff said, and my intention is to take his dead body back to Nottingham. Now, forester, can you lead me to the haunts of this Robin Hood?'

'I can, but I would advise you to be careful, Guy of Gisbourne, for I have heard that this Robin is a stout fighter. He might be more than a match for you.'

'More than a match for me! My advice to you is to watch your tongue, unless you would like to be tickled by my sword. I have heard that this outlaw has no taste for drawing blood, but I have no such scruples.'

'He is a great archer,' said Robin.

'I would challenge him – and beat him!'

'Will you challenge me then? I have a fair talent at archery, like all men of this county, though I admit I could not beat Robin Hood.'

Guy of Gisbourne gave a surly laugh. 'You've got spirit, fellow, that I will say. There are not many who have dared to challenge me. I warn you, after I have won I may kill you. Are you prepared for death?'

'When you have beaten me, you may kill me,' said Robin. With the outlaw watching him curiously, he cut a willow wand little thicker than a man's thumb, sharpened the point and set it in the ground. Then striding away from it for eighty paces, he called, 'Come, archer, split that wand in two.'

Guy looked at Robin, then at the target. 'It is not possible.'

'Surely you can achieve the impossible? If you are to capture and kill Robin Hood you will have to do just that!'

Guy strode to Robin's side and strung his bow in silence. His arrow missed the willow wand by a foot. Furious with himself, he tried again. His second arrow was only a little nearer than the first. He threw his bow down in disgust and clenched his fists. His eyes were full of black hatred.

'I will shoot now,' said Robin, 'and if you are not better with the broadsword than you are with bow and arrow, then Robin Hood will have no cause to worry.'

'Watch your tongue, oaf, or I may remove it for you.'

Robin ignored the threat and prepared to shoot. He fixed his eye on the target and released his first arrow. It swished across the eighty yards span and missed the willow by a mere inch. Guy of Gisbourne was startled by the nearness of the shot, but said nothing. Robin took aim with his second arrow and this time there was no error. The arrow passed right through the wand, splitting it in two. He grinned at Guy of Gisbourne, who was staring in disbelief.

'I am beginning to think that I am as good an archer as Robin Hood,' he said. 'Shall I now take you to him? How shall I introduce you? Guy of Gisbourne, thief, murderer, boaster, bully, a villain who betrays his fellow men for money – can you add to that list?'

Guy of Gisbourne growled like an animal at bay. 'Have a care if you want to live …' He drew his sword.

'And you have a care because you are going to die, Guy of Gisbourne. I am the Robin Hood you are looking for, the same Robin Hood who does not like to kill, unless it is to rid the earth of vermin such as you.' Robin's sword flashed in the sunlight.

They fought like men possessed, for each knew that one of them must die. Back and forth they went, till the grass was crushed beneath their trampling feet. Metal clanked as the swords met. Guy of Gisbourne was the

heavier, but Robin the quicker. More than once the point of Robin's sword felt the softness of flesh, and the ground began to be sprinkled with drops of blood. At last Robin gained the upper hand for his speed of movement had caused Guy to use up valuable energy, but at the moment when he felt sure of victory he caught his foot in a tree root and fell heavily on his back.

With a cry of glee Guy of Gisbourne leapt at him and stabbed at him with his sword. 'Dear Lady in Heaven, help me!' Robin cried, and caught the blade with his naked hand. Though it cut his palm the point plunged into the ground only inches from his side.

'Ah!' Guy wrenched his sword out and raised it again. But he had paused to take advantage of Robin's fall just a moment too long. Ignoring the blood pouring from his hand, Robin scrambled to his feet, and advanced on his opponent like an eagle on its prey. Guy looked round him wildly as if for protection, and in that instant Robin struck a back-handed blow beneath Guy's sword arm, which caused the weapon to drop from his grasp. Then he was exposed to the full fury of Robin's attack. His sword passed through the horse hide and straight into Guy's heart.

Guy of Gisbourne collapsed like a tree struck by lightning. With one shrill, wild cry he died at Robin's feet.

Robin, exhausted and dizzy, managed to wipe his sword and thrust it back into the scabbard. He stood over the dead man. His anger had disappeared and he felt only sadness. 'I did not want to kill you,' he said, 'but it had to be. Surely I have rid the world of an evil plague, and men will not blame me.'

He dragged the body into the bushes. 'The Sheriff of Nottingham sent this fiend to kill me,' he mused. 'Now I have another debt to settle. Perhaps if I change clothes with this fellow here I shall be in a better position to pay back what I owe.' He stripped Guy of Gisbourne of his horse-hide armour and put it on himself. He put his own cloak over the body and turned its face to the ground. Over it he spread fronds of bracken, so that from the path nothing of the dead man could be seen.

Then, pulling the horse-hood over his head, a different Guy of Gisbourne walked wearily through the forest.

The widow's sons

After parting from Robin Hood Little John went on his carefree way until he came to the high road, at the edge of which stood a small thatched cottage, half-hidden by an orchard of twisted apple trees. As he was passing by he heard the sound of weeping and, his tender heart ever ready to help someone in trouble, he left the road and hurried down the path until he reached the open door. Inside he saw an old woman sitting beside a fireless hearth. She was rocking herself backwards and forwards, sobbing bitterly.

She looked up at Little John with a tear-sodden face, and he patted her on the shoulder and begged her to tell him what her trouble was.

With many a gulp and sniff she did so. 'I have three fine sons,' she said, 'all the family left to me since my husband died, and today those three boys, the oldest only twenty years old, are all to be hanged.'

'Hanged?' said Little John. 'What have they done to deserve such a terrible fate?'

'Two of them have done nothing,' the woman said, 'but they refused to betray their eldest brother, and they are to die with him.'

'And he, the eldest?' asked Little John.

'He killed a deer. Oh, I know that he was breaking the law, but we have fallen on hard times and were near to starvation. The King's foresters followed a trail of blood to this cottage, and found the venison hanging up in the larder. They said that the Sheriff had sworn to check the slaughter of deer by hanging the first thief who was caught. My oldest son admitted that it was he alone who had killed the deer, but the other two refused to let him take all the blame. In the end they were all taken away, and I shall never see them again.' The old woman's tears began to flow again.

'Do you know where the lads have been taken?' asked Little John.

'To the *Saracen's Head* inn, at Southwell, for there the Sheriff is waiting the return of someone called Guy of Gisbourne he sent into Sherwood to catch Robin Hood. If he *is* caught, who then can poor people depend on?'

'Yours is a sad story,' said Little John, 'but all may not be lost.' I wonder what has been happening in the forest, he thought ... 'Have you any clothes I could wear in place of this Lincoln green?' he said aloud. 'If our brave Sheriff should see me as I am I shall join your sons on the gallows, I do not doubt. He does not love me as much as I would like him to!'

The woman rummaged in a cupboard and found some old clothes that had belonged to her husband. Little John put them on, then he asked her for some flour. He made his hair and beard white, rubbed dust on his cheeks, covered his head with a floppy hat, bade farewell to the old woman, and set out briskly for Southwell.

All was bustle and stir at the *Saracen's Head*, for the Sheriff and a score of his men were awaiting the return of Guy of Gisbourne. The Sheriff sat inside, the men were lounging outside under the shade of the trees in the courtyard. Their horses, with twitching tails and stamping feet, were tethered to a fence.

Three foresters approached, each pushing one of the widow's sons before him. They inquired where the Sheriff might be found, and marched into the inner room. One of them told their story. The three young men trembled at the Sheriff's fierce scowl and loud, angry voice.

'So you have been poaching the King's deer, have you? I will make short work of the three of you.'

'Sire, my brothers had nothing to do with it—' the eldest youth began.

'The three of you,' the Sheriff repeated, drowning the quavering tones. 'I will hang you all up as a farmer hangs up crows to scare the others. And when your bodies are swinging from a tree, I hope they will be an example to any other rogue who plans to do as you have done.' He turned to the foresters. 'I won't have them hanged here, as I have no wish to bring bad luck to the inn, but in Sherwood itself, where they committed their crime. Perhaps the news might reach the outlaws in the forest. Get me my horse.'

He and his men-at-arms mounted their horses. The three youths, still guarded by the foresters, walked behind the horsemen until they reached the outskirts of the forest, where stood a thick-limbed oak tree.

The guards fastened ropes around the youths' necks and flung the ends over a convenient bough. The eldest youth fell to his knees and begged for mercy for his brothers, but the Sheriff turned away indifferently.

'Mercy for none of you,' he said. 'I wish we had a priest here to hear your last confession, but as we have not you must trust to Saint Peter to let you into Paradise.'

While all this was going on an old man had drawn near and was watching the scene, leaning on his staff. Across his back was a yew bow that seemed too heavy for such a white-haired man to bear. The Sheriff beckoned to him. 'Who are you and what do you want?' he asked.

'I am just an old traveller who happens to be passing by,' the man said in a croaking voice. 'My name is Giles, and I come from Lincoln. I am on my way to visit my brother in Newark.'

'Would you like to earn yourself sixpence to help you on your way?' said the Sheriff. 'These three thieves are going to be hanged. If you will string them up I will give you two pence apiece for them. I do not want my own men to turn into hangmen. Will you do the job?'

'Well,' said the old man, 'I have never done such a thing before, but if sixpence is to be earned I might as well have it as anybody else. But, sire, are these men ready for death? Have they made their confession to God?'

'No,' said the Sheriff, 'but if you would like to act as priest too, and hear them, then you may do it for another two pence.'

'You are generous, my lord,' said the traveller, 'and I will do the job as well as I can.'

He went up to the first youth and put his ear to his cheek as though listening to whispered words of confession, but at the same time his own words fell softly into the youth's ear. 'I am a friend. My name is Little John. I am going to cut the rope, but stay as you are and do not move an inch. When you see me throw off my hat, then cast the noose from your neck and run into the forest as fast as you can.' Then he slyly cut the rope that bound the youth's hands and he, still trembling, but now with hope, grasped the cut end so that it should not fall and be seen. He stayed as he was, with bowed head and shoulders.

Then Little John moved to the second youth, and spoke the same words to him. The youth flushed with emotion and almost toppled over when he felt the rope being cut. But Little John steadied him, and then repeated his action with the youngest boy. He would have cried out, but Little John gave him a warning look, and the boy remained silent.

The Sheriff, a few yards away on his horse, thought it all a huge joke. 'You would make a good priest, old man, and I am sure that all their sins are now forgiven. Now let us see what kind of an executioner you make!'

Little John bobbed his head in humble salute. 'Please, my lord,' he said, 'will you give me leave to string my bow? For I would like to help these fellows on their way to Heaven with an arrow between the ribs when they are swinging aloft.'

'You are a bloodthirsty knave,' laughed the Sheriff. 'Yes, you may do that, but do not keep us long from our entertainment.'

Little John strung his bow so quickly and deftly that the surprised soldiers wondered how an old man could be so strong. Looking behind him to see that the way into the wood was clear, he suddenly threw off his hat, shouted 'Run!' at the top of his voice and, with the three youths at his side, dashed for the cover of the trees.

For a moment the Sheriff gazed after them in bewilderment, then he gave a roar. 'I know who that is – that accursed Little John! After him!'

Little John had almost reached the trees when he heard the babel of voices as the Sheriff and his men started in pursuit. 'Hurry,' he called to the youths. 'Do not wait for me. I will see you later.'

He turned to face the Sheriff. 'Stand back!' he called. 'The first man to move a step forward dies!'

The men-at-arms froze on the spot. In vain the Sheriff shouted at them, calling them cowards, urging them to go forward in a body. They would not move.

Little John slowly retreated backwards, and had almost reached safety when the Sheriff, beside himself with rage at the thought of losing his catch, spurred his horse and rode down on the outlaw as though he would trample him to the ground. Little John raised his bow and drew the arrow's feather to his cheek. But before he could loose the shaft, the bow that had served him well for so long split in his hands, and the arrow fell harmlessly at his feet.

The Sheriff's men raised a shout and came rushing at him. But before they could reach him the Sheriff himself had leaned from his horse and struck Little John with his sword. The outlaw ducked in time to avoid a direct blow but the flat of the blade crashed on to his head and he fell to the ground, his senses spinning.

The Sheriff's men crowded round, all with swords at the ready to finish him off, but the Sheriff restrained them. 'I am glad he did not die by my sword,' he said, 'for if ever a man deserved to die by hanging, it is he. See, he is beginning to stir.'

Little John opened his eyes and looked around him dazedly. His head felt as though a hammer was pounding away inside it. The soldiers seized him roughly, bound his hands behind him and lifted him up on to one of the horses, with his face to its tail and his feet strapped beneath its belly. Lolling to and fro like a rag doll, Little John was led back to the *Saracen's Head*. The only crumb of consolation his confused mind could dredge up was the fact that the widow's three sons had got away safely.

At the inn the Sheriff and his men celebrated the capture of Little John with drinking and laughter. 'This time tomorrow the rogue shall hang upon the gallows before the city gate,' the Sheriff boasted, and the soldiers banged on the table in approval. 'But what if the fellow should slip through my fingers between now and tomorrow?' he added. 'I would not have that happen for a thousand pounds. He has scores of friends who may be lurking about and who may try to rescue him. It may not be wise to wait until tomorrow. We will return to the tree from which he saved those three young villains, and he shall taste the medicine that they should have had.'

Once more they sat Little John on the horse, face to tail, and returned to the forest's edge. Out of the wood a man came hurrying, and the Sheriff turned sharply, sword in hand. But when he saw how the man was dressed he relaxed. 'That is Guy of Gisbourne!' he cried. 'He must have slain Robin Hood. Now we will slay his man, and the outlaw band will be as good as finished.'

Little John's heart seemed to crumble away inside him. He looked dully at the approaching figure and gave a groan. Not only were the man's clothes covered with blood, but Robin's horn was slung about him and he carried Robin's bow and broadsword. So Robin Hood, friend and master, was dead ... What use was it, then, for him to go on living? Let them get the hanging over and done with as soon as possible ...

The Sheriff's eyes were blazing with excitement. 'What luck have you had?' he cried. 'Your clothes are bloody. Does that mean—'

'If you do not like my clothes,' Robin Hood called back in a harsh voice like that of Guy of Gisbourne, 'then you may shut your eyes. The blood on me is that

of the vilest man who ever entered Sherwood Forest and whom I have slain today – though not without hurt to myself.'

'You wretch!' Little John burst out. 'You have killed the finest, gentlest man who ever lived. No man here was fit to touch the laces in his boots. Sherwood will never be the same again.' Tears rolled down his cheeks and his shoulders heaved. 'Kill me quickly so that I may join him …'

The Sheriff rubbed his hands. 'If what you say is true, it is the best day's work you are ever likely to do.'

'I do not lie,' said Robin in the same rough tone. 'See, is this not Robin Hood's sword, and this his bow, and this his horn? Do you think he would have given them to Guy of Gisbourne as a present?'

'Nay,' said the Sheriff, 'I believe you. Ask whatever you like of me, and it shall be yours. This is the happiest day of my life. The master dead and his right-hand man about to die.'

'The reward I want is neither money nor property,' said Robin, 'but the chance to kill the man as I have killed the master. Give this fellow's life into my hands, sire.'

The Sheriff was taken aback. 'I would have given you enough money for a knight's ransom. I was looking forward to pulling the rope round his neck myself, but you shall have him. The Sheriff of Nottingham always keeps his word.'

'Thank you.' Robin turned to the soldiers. 'Take the rogue down from the horse and prop him against the tree. I will soon show you how to stick a pig!'

There was some murmuring among the men at Robin's words. Though they did not care whether Little John were hanged or not, they did not like to see him butchered in cold blood, and especially by one whose reputation for cruelty had spread through many counties. Hanging was an accepted punishment for wrongdoing; killing by the sword was not part of a soldier's code, except in battle. But the Sheriff took no notice of his men's grumbling, and Little John was helped down from the horse.

While this was going on Robin Hood had fitted an arrow into both his bow and that of Guy of Gisbourne, then, when Little John had been taken to the tree, he drew a double-edged dagger.

'Stand back, all of you,' he ordered. 'You will spoil my pleasure if you get too close. You will make me nervous and I may miss his heart. Back, I say – further still. You will see well enough from a distance.'

The men fell back, not unwilling to put a good distance between them and this ruthless man. Some of them turned their faces away so that they should not witness what was about to happen. Only the Sheriff remained jubilant, anxious to see the dagger pierce Little John's heart.

Little John drew himself up to his full height as Robin Hood drew near, dagger in hand. 'Here is my breast, murderer,' he said scornfully. 'It is fitting that the hand that slew my dear master should slay me too.'

'Peace, Little John,' said Robin in a low voice. 'Do you not recognize me beneath this horse's hide?'

Little John gave no sign of the shock these words

caused, but his heart suddenly began to pound and his legs were so weak that he almost collapsed. 'Oh, Robin Hood …' he whispered.

'My bow and arrows lie over there, and my sword. I have this bow and dagger, so I am well armed too. Seize them as soon as I cut the rope. Now!'

The dagger slashed at Little John's bonds, and he was free. He leapt forward and caught up the bow and sword, and at the same moment Robin threw back the cowl from his face and bent Guy of Gisbourne's bow, with a barbed arrow fitted to the string.

'My Lord Sheriff,' he called, 'I have killed your man just as you wanted to kill mine. Take care that it is not your turn next. One step and your heart will stop beating for ever!' Seeing that Little John was at his side, bow and sword in hand, he put his horn to his lips and three loud blasts tore the air.

When the Sheriff of Nottingham saw whose face was revealed, and when the notes of the horn rang in his ears, he thought his last minutes had come.

'Robin Hood!' he shrieked, wheeled his horse round, and went off in a cloud of dust. His men, never thinking that they would ever see their proud master fleeing for his life, followed him in a confused rout. But, though he rode fast, he could not travel faster than one of Robin Hood's arrows. When he arrived at the gates of Nottingham, a grey goose shaft stuck out behind him like the tail feather of a moulting bird. For a long time afterwards he was forced to eat all his meals standing up, and lie in his bed face down to the pillow.

The rescue of Will

'I have tried law, and I have tried trickery, and I have failed in both,' mused the Sheriff of Nottingham. 'Guy of Gisbourne failed me. I have been made to look an ass. Somehow Robin Hood *must* be captured. I must see what can be done with the force of numbers.'

He called his officers together and told them what was in his mind. 'I want each of you to take four men with you, each group to a different part of the forest, and lie in wait for Robin Hood. But if any of you find yourselves outnumbered, sound your horn and all the others will rush to help you. To the man who is responsible for capturing this troublesome fellow I will give a hundred pounds, and twenty pounds for the capture of one of his men. Be bold, be crafty, and you will not fail.'

There were fifty officers, each with four men, who went into Sherwood Forest, each officer determined to find the outlaw and win the prize for himself. For a week they hunted through the forest glades but never saw a single man in Lincoln green, for news of the man-hunt had reached Robin Hood by way of Arthur Fletcher, the landlord of the *Black Swan* inn at Edwin-stowe, who was a secret admirer of the outlaw, and whose son was a member of the band.

'If the Sheriff dares to send force to meet force,' Robin said grimly to the assembled outlaws, 'then there will be trouble, and blood will flow. I would rather shun battle and bloodshed because of the sorrow it would bring to the wives and children of the slain, and we will stay silently in the forest in case our pursuers decide to give up the hunt. But if we are forced to defend ourselves, then it is every man for himself. Make sure you are never without your bow and your broadsword.'

Many of the men were doubtful of the wisdom of this course, and David of Doncaster spoke up for them. 'The Sheriff will think we are cowards, and folk in the countryside will scoff at us and say we are frightened to meet the Sheriff's men. Cannot we come out in the open and engage them in battle without further delay?'

But Robin would not be turned from his plan. 'It would be best if they got tired of looking for us and went home empty-handed,' he said. 'Do not forget, if there is a fight, some of you might be killed, and I cannot have any death on my conscience. Only once have I killed and that was something that could not be avoided. I will send one of you to go and find out what the Sheriff's men are up to, and where they are, then I will decide what our next move will be. Will Stutely, you are as sly as an old dog fox, you shall go!'

Will Stutely was delighted. As a man of action he had chafed under the need to lie low and remain hidden. He dressed himself in one of Friar Tuck's habits, and under it he hung a sword round his waist. After some hours of careful reconnaisance he came to the edge of the forest where he struck the dusty highway that led to Nottingham. Before he reached Edwinstowe he saw two bands of the Sheriff's men but ignored them, and because they were not interested in a wandering preacher they took no notice of him. When he reached the small village he made for the *Black Swan* so that he could get the latest news from the landlord.

At the inn, however, he came across more of the men, sitting on benches outside and drinking. They seemed tired and dispirited. Will sat down on another bench, as far away from them as possible, waiting until he could have a word with the landlord in private. Arthur Fletcher, not recognizing Will as one of Robin's men, left him alone and neither spoke to him nor served him with beer, for he did not like priests and holy men.

As Will sat there, wondering when it would be possible to gain the landlord's ear, a black cat wandered up to him and rubbed against his leg, so that the friar's robe was accidentally lifted up a few inches, revealing a leg covered in green hose. Will pushed the robe down quickly, but not before one of the officers had got a glimpse of the unfamiliar colour.

'That is no holy friar,' the man thought. 'I wonder if he is one of the men we are after.' He went over to the grey-clad figure, his face hidden by a cowl, and said, 'Will you take a pot of ale to slake your thirst, holy father? You seem to have come a good way and look tired.'

Will shook his head silently.

'Where are you going on this hot day?' the officer persisted.

'I am a pilgrim on my way to Canterbury,' Will said in a hoarse voice, wishing that the man were not so curious.

'I do not think you will reach Canterbury,' the officer said, and chuckled in a way that sent a shiver down Will's spine. 'Do pilgrims usually wear Lincoln green beneath their robes? Could it be, by any chance, that you are one of Robin Hood's men?'

'I—' Will began.

'Do not move!' the officer cried, 'or I will run you through the body with my sword!'

He pointed it at Will's heart, but Will sprang up, jumped up on the bench and, before the astonished officer knew what was happening, he had withdrawn his own sword, and the two sharp points were level.

The officer struck, but Will parried the blow and got one in of his own that brought the man down to his knees, bleeding from a wound in the shoulder. But as he crashed he fell against the bench which overturned, bringing Will down with it, and the officer seized him by the legs and held on grimly. Will's sword flew wide, and the two men rolled on the ground, struggling fiercely.

For Will it was soon over. The officer's companions rushed up, parted the two men, and overpowered him. Soon he was bound hand and foot and led away. The landlord and his daughter stood gazing helplessly after him.

'If only I had known that it was Will Stutely,' Arthur Fletcher muttered, 'this would not have happened. Molly, you must run into the forest, find Robin Hood and tell him that brave Will has been taken.'

Robin Hood was talking to Little John and Friar Tuck when he saw Much the miller's son and David of Doncaster approaching, supporting between them a red-faced girl who appeared almost on the point of collapse. 'We found Molly from the inn looking for you,' Much explained. 'I fear she has sad news.'

'About Will?' Robin's face paled.

'Will has been taken,' Molly said, the tears streaming down her face. 'The Sheriff's men have bound him and taken him away to Nottingham. I heard one of them say that he will be hanged tomorrow. Oh, sir, you must save him!'

'Will hanged?' Robin cried. 'Never! The Sheriff will have cause to regret what he has done today.' He clapped his horn to his lips. Soon he was surrounded by his outlaws who, when they heard the news, growled with anger and swore vengeance on those who had taken Will Stutely.

'Listen to me,' Robin said. 'Tomorrow I shall go to Nottingham and bring Will Stutely back to the forest – or I shall die with him. He has risked life and limb for us. Who is ready to come with me and risk life and limb for him?'

There was a great shout. 'I am!' came from a hundred throats, for there was not one man who would not venture everything for a friend in need.

Early the next morning the outlaws left the forest in small groups by a dozen different routes. Robin Hood had given them their orders. They were to lie in ambush outside the gates of Nottingham in a small wood known as Mapperley Copse until they received news of what was happening in the town; then final plans could be made. They lay hidden for a long time, and it was almost midday when Robin Hood, seeing that the road was empty except for an old man walking slowly from the direction of the town, sent David of Doncaster to question the traveller.

David slipped out of the copse and hailed the old man who, from his dress, appeared to be a pilgrim such as Will Stutely had pretended to be. 'Good morrow, holy father,' he said. 'Can you give me news from Nottingham? Is it true that Will Stutely is to be hanged on the gallows today? I would not care to miss such a sight for I have come a long way to see the rogue meet the end he deserves.'

'Alas,' the pilgrim answered sadly, 'it is true enough, and it is a sorry thing. I have passed the very spot where the gallows tree is going up, at a point where three roads meet just outside the town. He is to be hanged just as the sun goes down. I could not bear the sight, so I have come away.' Then he added, with a flash of anger, 'I am sorry you have come to enjoy yourself. Though Will Stutely is an outlaw in Robin Hood's band, yet he takes only from the rich and dishonest. Many a poor widow and many a humble peasant have cause to bless Robin Hood's name, for he will see nobody hungry or in trouble if he can do anything about it. If only Robin Hood were here now ...'

'Thank you for your news, old man,' David of Doncaster said. 'Maybe Robin Hood is not so far away, and what I really came to enjoy is not the sight of Will Stutely hanging, but riding away to safety, with the Sheriff and his men in disarray. Fare you well, father. May you always think well of outlaws.'

He ran back to the wood, leaving the old pilgrim looking after him curiously.

'We had better go into the city now,' said Robin, 'and mix with the people. There are sure to be great crowds and we shall not be noticed. Make sure you keep in sight of one another, get as near to Will and his guards as you can when they leave the gate. Do not strike anybody without cause because we want to avoid bloodshed, but if you do have to fight, fight hard so that you do not have to give a second blow. Once again, heed my warning – keep together!'

The sun was low in the western sky when a single bugle note was heard from the castle wall. In the town all was bustle and noise, as though it were Goose Fair time. Crowds thronged the narrow streets. It was not every day that a public hanging took place, and the citizens were determined to regard it as a public holiday. The fact that the victim was a leading member of the outlaw band gave an added excitement to the affair.

Presently the castle gates opened and a great array of men-at-arms came out, the Sheriff at their head, dressed in shining mail of linked chain. In the middle of the soldiers, standing in a cart drawn by four oxen, with a noose already round his neck, rode Will Stutely. His face was pale, his hair matted with blood, his eyes dark with despair. He looked around him for familiar faces but, though some people showed pity and some friendliness, he saw nobody he knew, and his heart was like lead. There was no help from any quarter.

When the procession stopped, Will spoke up boldly. 'My Lord Sheriff,' he said, 'not one of Robin Hood's men has ever died upon a tree, and I do not wish to be the first. Grant me my sword and let me die fighting. I am only one against all your pikemen and archers, and I shall only do but little harm.'

'Your request is dismissed,' the Sheriff said coldly. 'You shall die the death of a criminal.'

'Please,' Will begged, 'if I cannot have my sword, then let me fight with my bare fists.'

'Enough!' cried the Sheriff. 'You shall die where three roads meet, so that all can see you and take warning from your fate. I mean everyone to know what will happen to Robin Hood and all his men when they are caught, as caught they will be.'

'You lie!' Will said. 'Robin Hood will never be caught! He scorns you and cowards like you. Your name will evermore go down as one with the blackest heart in Christendom.'

The Sheriff's face darkened and he muttered a curse, but did not argue further with the defiant prisoner. He spurred his horse forward and they came to the town gate. Beyond was the countryside, with hills and dales now misty with the evening, and Will could see the dusky line of Sherwood's trees. There were sheep bleating nearby, and birds were making their night calls. Will's eyes blurred with tears. This is the last time I shall see my beloved country, he thought. He bowed his head so that the onlookers should not think him unmanly.

The procession arrived at the point where the three

roads met. The cart was led to its destination beneath the gallows and came to a halt. A sudden silence fell upon the crowd. Expectant, uneasy, people did not know what to say, how to act.

Will, now that the end was near, lifted his head. He glanced from side to side so that all should see he was not afraid. Then his heart lurched violently in his chest, and he could scarcely keep from calling out. There in the press of people was Robin Hood, looking at him gravely, nodding as though to say that his ordeal would soon be over. And not far away was Little John ... and near him Will Scarlet ... and Much the miller's son ... and Arthur-a-Bland ... and David of Doncaster ...

Man after man he recognized, behind the line of men-at-arms, and all were his friends. Suddenly hope flooded into him. They had come to set him free – but how could they? The odds against them were too great, they could never break through the line of pikemen.

Then there was a great movement in the crowd, a surge forward like waves breaking on the seashore. The outlaws were pushing the people in front of them forward, and were in turn being pushed by others behind so that it seemed as if the chief actors in the drama would be swallowed by a press of bodies and disappear from sight.

The Sheriff was getting anxious. 'Stand back!' he shouted. 'Get back, all of you! Stop pushing, you will have us all down!'

But the tidal wave of people moved relentlessly forward. The pikemen linked arms and tried to restrain the seething mass, but could not. Their line broke and they toppled over like ninepins.

'Back! Back!' roared the Sheriff, but nobody heard him.

Robin Hood had jumped on to the cart. A soldier swung his sword at him but Robin dodged nimbly and the weapon whistled harmlessly past his ears. He leapt to Will's side and with his knife cut the rope that bound his arms and lay around his neck. 'Jump down,' Robin hissed. 'I will follow. Mingle with the crowd.'

Will obeyed and was soon lost to view. Robin next addressed himself to the Sheriff, whose horse had knocked several people down as he reached the cart. He had risen in his stirrups with his sword raised above his head.

'What, Sir Sheriff?' he mocked. 'Have you come to take Will Stutely's place on the gallows?' He danced backwards and forwards while the Sheriff lunged at him in vain. The horse was whinnying with fright and rearing up so that the Sheriff was hardly able to keep his balance.

Robin roared with laughter. 'Try again, sire,' he cried, 'but you will not find it as easy as you thought to hack Robin Hood to pieces!'

'Treason!' panted the Sheriff. 'You have robbed the gallows of one rogue, but another shall take his place.'

As he spoke an arrow flew past his head, missing him by only an inch. A score more followed, all carefully aimed to miss him, but near enough to make him flinch in terror and at last drop his sword. Around him a battle was raging. Swords clashed, there were shouts, oaths and groans as the Sheriff's men, outnumbered by the outlaws, began to fall back. The people of Nottingham scuttled out of harm's way. When they realized that Robin Hood was among them they shouted and cheered as though they were watching a tournament arranged specially for their enjoyment.

The Sheriff had to admit defeat. With a despairing gesture he turned his horse and galloped away, followed by as many of his men as were not lying on the ground nursing their wounds.

'Let him go, men,' Robin called, and the sorry band disappeared into the distance with a shower of arrows to help them in their flight.

Will Stutely made his way back to Robin's side and clutched his arm. 'Oh, master,' he said, 'you are a true friend. Little did I think I would see your face today, or meet you again this side of Paradise. What can I say to thank you?'

Robin patted Will on the shoulder. 'Why, nothing,' he said cheerfully. 'It is I who should thank you. I shall always remember this day with pleasure. I fancy the Sheriff will leave us alone now he realizes once again how near he came to losing his life. He will not be able to face his people for many a week, he will be so ashamed of the ass he made of himself trying to hang one of Robin Hood's men.'

The outlaws returned to the forest in high spirits. Tired though they were, they laughed and sang, and as the darkness swallowed them up the echoes of their voices lingered round the stone walls of the city.

Robin Hood and the Bishop

Robin Hood had grown a little careless, which was not like him. His success in rescuing Will Stutely and defeating the Sheriff made him think that it would be safe to leave the forest and wander abroad without fear of meeting an enemy. 'The Sheriff is a coward as well as a bully,' he said to Little John, 'and for the time being we can relax our guard and venture further afield. It will be good to show ourselves to people and let them know that we are not as bad as the Sheriff makes out.'

Little John was doubtful. 'The Sheriff is not our only

enemy,' he said. 'There are many men of high degree who would dearly love to see us clapped into prison. I can think of half a dozen bishops and abbots.'

But Robin remained optimistic. 'They care more for their own skin than even the Sheriff does,' he said. 'Do not worry, friend. We will not take unnecessary risks, but I do feel that a short holiday from care will do us all good. It can be irksome being confined to the forest all the time.'

The next day Robin was strolling along the high road quite openly. There was nobody in sight, neither friend nor foe, and he was whistling merrily, slashing at the tall grasses at the roadside with his staff, thinking about nothing in particular, enjoying the feeling of freedom. He approached a sharp bend in the road, rounded it without taking his usual precautions, and stopped short in utter amazement.

Perched on a horse almost as fat as himself, and in company with a large number of the Sheriff of Nottingham's men, was the Bishop of Hereford.

Robin's whistle trailed into silence. 'Here's a pretty kettle of fish,' he said to himself. 'He hates me for the trick I played at Allan-a-Dale's wedding, and I dislike him because he is greedy and cruel. I wonder what he will try to do ...'

When the Bishop recognized the man standing before him he was glad he had brought the Sheriff's men with him for protection while travelling through this part of the county. He had had a feeling that he might come across some of the outlaws and was determined to be prepared.

The two men stared at each other for a few moments, then the Bishop gave an exultant shout. 'You will not get away this time, my fine friend!' He prodded his horse and moved towards Robin. It was too late for Robin to retreat the way he had come so, quick as a flash, he dived off the road, dodged under some bushes, and disappeared so suddenly that the earth might have swallowed him up.

The Bishop had no intention of following Robin into the forest. He did not know how many of his friends might be lurking about, ready to pick him off with an arrow, but on the other hand he was determined not to lose the advantage of surprising Robin when he was alone. 'After him!' he shouted to the soldiers. 'Some of you beat up the woods around him. Some of you double back in case he should try to escape further down the road. The rest, stay here with me to catch him when he is flushed out.'

The men did not have much heart for an encounter with the dreaded outlaws, but they obeyed the Bishop without question, and the search was on.

Robin did not have much of a start, but he knew the forest intimately, and he had not spent many years in it without learning some of the ways of the animals – how to conceal himself by merging into the background, and how to move silently through the undergrowth. He knew where he was making for, and he was sure he would get there before his pursuers. Their shouts and the thud of their feet were still very much in evidence, but they were not getting any nearer, and Robin knew that he would reach his destination with a few minutes to spare.

He gave a gasp of relief when he came in sight of the old stone cottage between forest and highway that was the home of the old widow whose three sons had been saved from the gallows by Little John. He knew that she would help him if she could, and as he ran the last hundred yards he hastily thought up a plan of campaign.

He jumped over the rickety fence into the orchard and dashed up the path. He poked his head in through the open window.

The old woman, who was at her spinning-wheel, jumped up with a cry of alarm and crossed herself. 'Oh, mercy, sir, whoever you are! What do you want?'

'Hush, good woman! I have not come to harm you. Do you not recognize me? I am Robin Hood.' Robin gave a quick look behind him. There was nobody in sight yet.

She peered at him shortsightedly, then nodded her head and smiled. 'Good Robin Hood, you are welcome. Come inside and I will find you food.'

'I have no time,' Robin replied. 'Tell me, where are your sons?'

'They are all out working. Since your friend saved them things have gone well for us. We owe you a debt we can never repay.'

'I have come to take repayment of that debt. I need your help desperately. The Bishop of Hereford and some of the Sheriff's men are seeking me. A gang of them are on my heels and will soon be here. Will you help me?'

'You need not ask! We will cheat the Bishop some-how! But alas, I cannot hide you here, there is no safe place of concealment.' The widow bent her brows in thought. 'I know! You can be hidden in full view of them all ...'

'How can that be? Robin asked.

'Quickly, pass me your clothes through the window, and I will give you mine. You can be an old widow woman, and I a bold outlaw.' While she was speaking she had taken off her grey cloak and was unfastening her petticoat.

Robin could not imagine that her plan would succeed, but it was the only possible thing to do. He dragged his clothes off and threw them through the window, together with his bow, sword and knife. In return he received cloak, petticoat, shoes, the spindle of the spinning-wheel, and a dark, gnarled walking stick. In no time he had transformed himself. He felt very strange and wondered how successful his disguise would be.

But there was no more time for wondering. From the forest came the Sheriff's men and with them the Bishop, red-faced and panting, who had decided that after all he must be in at the kill and would risk the hazards of the forest. They all stopped before the cottage and looked around them. All they could see was a bent old woman with a shawl about her head, stumbling along with the aid of a stick and muttering to herself as she went.

'You there, crone,' said the Bishop haughtily. 'Have you seen Robin Hood around here?'

'Eh?' said the woman, cupping a hand to her ear.

'Robin Hood – the outlaw – have you seen him?'

'Mind your own business, it is nothing to do with you who I see or don't see.'

The Bishop's fury increased at a humble peasant daring to address him in such a way. 'Have a care,' he growled, 'or you will find yourself in the stocks.'

'Then I will put a curse on you. Do you hear? A curse. I care not who you are. You have no right to prevent an old woman from going about her business.'

The Bishop was speechless with rage. One of the soldiers touched Robin gently on the shoulder.

'Take your hands off me! I have done nothing to be bullied by a soldier or threatened by a fat priest.'

'Come, come, my good woman,' the soldier said soothingly, 'nobody is going to harm you. This is my

Lord Bishop of Hereford and all he wants to know is if you have seen Robin Hood hereabouts.'

'Aye, that I have, and a fine fair sight he is too. I've seen Robin Hood, and I've seen you, and I've seen that fat pig you say is a Bishop, and I've seen cats and dogs and foxes and hares and hedgehogs and deer—'

'Quiet, you doltish crone!' The Bishop's teeth were chattering. 'We do not want a list of everything you have seen. It is Robin Hood we are seeking. If you know where he is, then say so, or I will have you burned as a witch.'

At that Robin pretended to give way to fear. 'Mercy, mercy! Not that, please! I am no witch, only an old woman trying to live in peace with the little food I can find and the bit of work my bent and tired fingers can do. What law is it that says Robin Hood cannot visit me with a fresh young rabbit for my dinner? He is a good man and always welcome at my cottage.'

'Ah!' The Bishop pricked up his ears. 'He is in your cottage now, is he?'

'Oh, what have I said?' Robin's mumble turned to a shrill squeak. 'Who told you that he is in my cottage?'

'You said so yourself, stupid woman,' said the Bishop. 'We will now flush the rat from the trap, then we will deal with you.'

'You will never take him alive!'

'We will see about that. Get into the cottage, men. Burn it down, if need be. Do anything, but get Robin Hood. I'll give a purse of gold pieces to the man who captures the outlaw alive.'

As the men dashed towards the cottage they did not

notice the old woman hobbling towards the forest. Nor did they see how, the further away from them she got, the swifter and straighter grew her pace, the bent back became upright, and, once inside the shelter of the trees, how she broke into a swift run.

Robin sped along familiar paths. Thankfully he saw some of his friends in the distance. Little John, Arthur-a-Bland and one or two others were chopping branches for firewood in a little clearing. They looked up at the sound of running footsteps.

'Look at that,' said Little John. 'Who could believe an old woman could run so fast! Perhaps she is a witch riding an invisible broomstick! Witch or woman, I think I will send an arrow close to her head.'

The supposed woman came to a stop a few yards from them and raised one hand. 'Don't shoot! It is I, Robin Hood!' Robin was so out of breath he could scarcely get the words out. 'Call all the men at once. You who are here come with me. The Bishop of Hereford at this very moment thinks he is settling a score with me. With luck, we shall settle one with him instead.'

When Little John could stop laughing he blew his horn. 'Now, mistress Robin, lead on. We are right behind you. Mind you pick up your skirts well!'

Back at the widow's cottage the Bishop was not finding it easy to capture Robin Hood. The men were having difficulty in breaking down the door, but finally, with the aid of a tree trunk, it was rammed and burst open. The men stood guard on the threshold. From a safe distance the Bishop called upon Robin Hood to come out. When there was no reply he ordered the men to go in. 'Why do you hesitate?' he said. 'There are twenty of you and only one of him.'

But not one man dared to enter for fear an arrow should meet him half-way. One of them peered into the gloom. 'There he is,' he cried. 'I see him in the corner by the cupboard. He seems to be crouching down. Shall we kill him with our pikes?'

'No, take him alive if you can. I have waited a long time to see him hanged. What an occasion that will be!' Now that his moment of triumph was so near the Bishop had recovered his good humour, and his fat cheeks were creased with a smile.

But his joy was short-lived. From behind the cottage appeared the shabby figure of the old woman who had caused him so much trouble, and she was evidently very angry. She began to scold the soldiers in high-pitched tones.

'Stand aside, you villains! Which of you broke down my cottage door? Who gave orders to destroy my home?' She turned to the Bishop, shaking her fist. 'Was it you?'

'Hold your tongue, woman,' cried the distracted Bishop. 'If you harbour thieves and outlaws then you must think yourself lucky your house is not burned to the ground. The men are obeying my orders and they will go on doing so.'

'Things have come to a pretty pass when a poor widow-woman's home is not safe from rogues of priests. Could you not catch one man without all this fuss? Soldiers! You are rather simpering maidens! You are cowards who deserve the curse I shall put on you!'

'Seize the hag!' the Bishop shouted as soon as he could get in a word. 'We will take her back with us, and she will be punished as a witch, as Robin Hood will be for his ungodly behaviour.'

'Ungodly behaviour is a fine thing for you to talk about,' the old woman retorted. 'A good joke you have made, and I will clap my hands to applaud you.'

And at the signal a large number of outlaws appeared from behind the trees that surrounded the cottage, each with his bow strung. The Bishop saw that he was trapped again. With a last effort to keep control of the situation, he called out, 'If one of you comes one inch closer, or looses one arrow, your master will die! My men have their pikes ready, and I shall command them to kill him. Robin Hood will not leave that cottage alive!'

A clear voice came from under the widow's shawl. 'I should like to see the Robin Hood you have caught in the cottage, my lord. For I am the only Robin Hood I know, and there are no pikes threatening me. But are there two of us? Have I a namesake, or a rival, or perhaps a long-lost twin brother? Who is it you are guarding so thoroughly?'

As one man the Bishop and the soldiers slowly turned their heads to the cottage door. Out came the real widow, on whose small spare body Robin's clothes looked absurd. His jacket reached to her knees and his cap almost covered her head. 'My Lord Bishop,' she piped. 'I welcome you to my humble abode. Have you come to bless me and give me a few pieces of gold for my comfort?'

'Well spoken, good mother,' Robin said. 'He is going to pay for a new door too. Is that not so, sire?'

'By all the saints—' the Bishop began, then stumbled into silence.

'Those same saints who are watching you now,' said Robin. 'So do not call on them with your ungodly lips. As you seem in no hurry to pay for the damage you have done, I will trouble you to hand over the purse of gold you promised for my capture.' He held out his hand.

The Bishop retreated a step. Black rage was on his face. His lips moved silently, as though the words he wanted to say would not come out. His whole body quivered. Never before had his dignity been so outraged. When at last he could speak, the words were like cold pebbles rattling to the ground. 'Never! You will get no gold from me. All you will get is a rope around your neck. Have at them, men. Hew them down in their tracks. Leave only this man for us to take away.'

'Not so fast,' said Robin, 'for it is *we* who have *you* at our mercy.' He took a bow from the nearest outlaw and aimed an arrow that whistled so close to the Bishop's head that it took away his skull cap and exposed his bald head.

The Bishop turned as white as his shiny scalp and clutched wildly at his ears as though he thought they had gone too. Then he threw his hands in the air. 'Mercy!' he gasped. 'Do not shoot me! You shall have your gold, but do not shoot!' He fumbled in the folds of his cloak and took out a bulging purse. He tossed it over to Robin.

With all his dignity gone he hurried away from the cottage as fast as his short legs could carry him. The soldiers followed him in sullen retreat. They had no leader and saw no point in risking their lives without good cause.

Robin's men began to make temporary repairs to the widow's door while she and Robin sat at her table counting the gold pieces which were her reward for her courageous help.

King Richard visits Sherwood

All Nottinghamshire was in a stir and tumult, for King Richard was making a royal progress through England, and he was to stay for a few days in Nottingham as a guest of the Sheriff.

Preparations for entertaining the King were quickly set in hand. Great wooden arches were built across the streets and draped with banners and streamers and decorated with flowers. In the Guildhall the best silver plate was taken out and polished, for a magnificent banquet was to be given. Dancers practised their steps and minstrels their songs. The sky was scanned anxiously to forecast the weather, and when the day of the visit arrived, bright sun flooded the scene. The streets and squares were packed with people as tightly as herrings in a box. The Sheriff's men, halberds in hands, had difficulty in clearing a space for the royal visitors to ride through on their horses.

'Take care who you are pushing,' said a burly friar to one of the soldiers, and a shout of laughter came from a number of green-clad yeomen who were scattered through the crowd. But one of them nudged the holy man with his elbow. 'Peace, Tuck,' he said sharply. 'You promised me you would put a check on your tongue. We want to *see* the procession, not hear it from the darkness of a dungeon.'

'Sorry, master,' said Friar Tuck.

Everybody fell silent when the clear sound of bugle horns came from the town's main gate. Twenty-eight heralds in velvet and cloth of gold came first, each carrying a silver trumpet. From each trumpet hung a banner with the royal arms of England emblazoned on it. After the trumpeters a hundred noble knights cantered by, two by two, all fully armed. From their lances fluttered many-coloured pennons. Each knight was accompanied by a page, and each page carried his master's helmet with its floating plume of feathers.

Behind the King's knights came the barons and nobles of the midland counties, then a great array of men-at-arms, with spears and halberds in their hands. They were escorting two riders. One was the Sheriff of Nottingham in his robes of office. The other, taller than the Sheriff, his fair beard shot with grey, his keen blue eyes glinting, was King Richard the Lionheart, beloved by his people for his bravery in the Holy Land and for his wisdom and kindness at home. He bowed to the right and to the left, and a mighty roar of cheering followed him.

The noise was increased by a voice roaring, 'Heaven bless our gracious King Richard! All the saints bless our noble King!' Looking down, the King saw an immensely fat priest at the edge of the crowd, his legs wide apart, clapping wildly.

The King could not help laughing. 'By my soul, Sheriff,' he said, 'you have more strapping priests in your county than I've ever seen in my life! That man would make a stone image of Saint Peter rub its ears. I would not mind an army of such men.'

When the Sheriff saw who the priest was his face turned white, and he had to catch the pommel of his saddle to keep from swaying. He gave a faint moan when nearby he saw Robin Hood, Little John, Will Scarlet, Will Stutely and others of the outlaw band.

'What is the matter, Sheriff?' the King asked. 'You have gone very pale.'

'It is only a pain that will soon pass,' the Sheriff replied. Beneath his alarm was a fierce anger. Robin Hood fears me so little, he thought, that he dares to come right into the town and show his face openly.

At the end of an exhausting day the Guildhall feast was held. There were mountains of food and the wine flowed freely. The vast room was lit by a thousand wax tapers, and King Richard sat at the head of the table on a throne all hung with cloth of gold.

'I have heard much about the doings of an outlaw called Robin Hood,' he said idly to his host. 'I believe that you have had dealings with him more than once. Tell me about him, Sir Sheriff.'

The Sheriff looked down without speaking, sensing that the King was making fun of him, but the Bishop of Hereford, sitting on the King's other side, said bitterly, 'He is the boldest law-breaker with the blackest heart in the country, Your Majesty. It is time the villain was brought to justice.'

There was a murmur of agreement from some of the Sheriff's friends, but young Sir Henry of the Lea, who had fought for the King in the Holy Land, spoke up. 'My father, Sir Richard of the Lea, knows this fellow well, Your Majesty, and has told me many stories about him that show him in a much better light. My father thinks the world of him.'

'I bid you tell us the tale,' said the King, seeing the black looks that the Sheriff and the Bishop were giving the young man, and smiling inwardly.

'My father once owed the Bishop here four hundred pounds,' said Sir Henry. 'He called the money in at a very inconvenient time, and would not grant my father time to pay. The result was that he was left without any means at all. One day, riding through Sherwood Forest, with empty purse and shabby clothes, he was captured by Robin Hood, who thought he would take a handsome fee from him to pay for the feast he was invited to. But when no money was forthcoming and Robin Hood heard what had happened, he loaned my father four hundred pounds of his own money for an indefinite period and with no interest, and my father was sent on his way rejoicing. Soon afterwards the outlaws came upon the Bishop and forced him to go with them to their hideout. In payment for the dinner he had to yield up the same amount that he had taken from my father! Many months later, when my father's fortunes were restored, he returned to the forest to repay the loan, only to be told that it had already been paid. So you see, Your Majesty, my family has cause to bless this bold law-breaker, and the Bishop has cause to curse him!'

The King and his friends were highly amused. The Bishop had to bite his lip to prevent himself from saying something he might regret.

'Robin Hood is indeed a bold and merry fellow,' said the King, 'even though I hear he is not above poaching my deer. I would give a hundred pounds to meet him and see what he gets up to in Sherwood Forest.'

'You would do better, sire, to give your money to the Church,' said the Bishop sourly.

That night the King sat in his lodgings in the castle, talking over the events of the day with some of his nobles. Robin Hood's name was mentioned again, and Sir Henry of the Lea said, 'If Your Majesty is really anxious to meet Robin Hood and perhaps lose a hundred pounds, I can arrange for you to meet him and feast with him in the forest.'

'How can you do that, lad?' smiled the King.

'Will you put yourself in my hands, sire?'

'Aye, you shall rule me for once, and I will be your subject.'

'Then,' said Sir Henry eagerly, 'let Your Majesty and the six of us here put on robes of the Order of Black Friars, and let Your Majesty hide a purse of one hundred pounds beneath your gown. We will ride from here to Mansfield and, unless I am much mistaken, we shall meet Robin Hood and be asked to dine with him. What happens after that we will leave to chance, but I reckon there will be much sport.'

Early the next morning the seven men, dressed in the habits of the Black Friars, slipped out of the castle before the Sheriff and his household were awake, mounted their horses and rode out of the town. They travelled through the open country between bare fields for several miles along the road to Mansfield without seeing a soul, and when they had almost reached the little town, the King reined his horse.

'Has anyone brought anything to drink?' he asked. 'My throat is parched.'

His men shook their heads. 'We did not think of it, sire,' one of them said.

The King sighed. 'I would give fifty pounds to be able to quench my thirst.'

Hardly had he spoken when a man appeared, as if from nowhere, and laid his hand on the King's bridle rein. He was tall, with yellow hair and a pair of merry blue eyes. 'Forgive me, holy brother,' he said, 'but I could not help hearing what you said. It would be un-christian not to try to help you. We keep an inn nearby, and for fifty pounds we will not only give you as much wine as you can drink but also a feast that the King himself would be proud to sit down to.' He gave a piercing whistle, the bushes at the roadside swayed and crackled, and at least fifty broad-shouldered men in Lincoln green burst into view.

'How now, fellow,' said the King, not quite as surprised as he appeared to be. 'Who are you? Have you no regard for holy men?'

'None at all,' said Robin Hood, 'for all the holiness that rich friars have could be put into a thimble. As for my name – you may have heard of Robin Hood.'

'A bold fellow, and a lawless one, so I'm told,' said the King. 'Pray you, let me and my holy brothers pass by in peace.'

'No, no,' said Robin, 'for it would never do to let holy men travel with empty stomachs. I expect that between you there is a well-filled purse that will pay for the wine we offer. Show it to me, whoever has it, or I shall have to strip all your robes from you and find it myself.'

The King looked stern. 'There is no need for threats. Here is the purse,' and he took it from beneath his habit. 'I charge you not to lay hands on me or any of my brothers.'

'Proud words!' said Robin. 'Are you the King of England to talk in that way? Will, take the purse and count the contents.'

Will Scarlet counted the money. 'One hundred pounds,' he said. 'A rich friar indeed.'

Robin took fifty of the gold pieces and put the other fifty back in the purse, and handed it back to the King. 'Thank the saints that you have fallen into the hands of gentle rogues,' he said, grinning. 'Now, brothers, will you not put back your cowls? I like to see the faces of my guests.'

'No,' said the King. 'We have all vowed that we shall not show our faces to the world for twenty-four hours, and I beg you to allow us to keep our vow.'

'I will grant your request,' said Robin. 'Now we will lead you to our inn where you may drink your fill.' He called seven of his men, who each took a horse by the bridle. They turned off the road, crossed several fields until they reached the forest, and eventually the outlaws' hideout. Robin was surprised at the lack of protest from his victims, but decided that perhaps they were not as arrogant as most priests.

When they arrived at the clearing they found Friar Tuck and about two dozen outlaws waiting to see who Robin had brought back. Little John and the rest were searching another part of the forest for a rich guest.

King Richard dismounted and looked about him with interest. 'You have in truth a fine lot of young men about you, Robin Hood. King Richard himself would be glad of such a bodyguard.'

'These are not all,' Robin said proudly. 'Little John, my right-hand man, is away on business with the rest of them. As for King Richard, brother, there is not one of us who would not pour out blood like water for him. We outlaws love him dearly. His courage is an example to us all.'

'He would like to hear you say that, I am sure,' said the King.

Friar Tuck bustled up to them. 'Good day to you,

brothers. I am glad to welcome some of my cloth to this secret place.'

'Who are you, mad priest?' said the King. 'I do not recognize you.'

Friar Tuck turned to Robin. 'Never again let me hear you say that I am not a patient man. A knave of a friar has called me a mad priest, and I have not knocked him to the ground! My name is Friar Tuck, brother, a member of your order, and yet not a member, if you understand me.'

'That is enough, Tuck,' Robin said. 'Bring some wine. These gentlemen are thirsty, and since they have already paid for it they must have it straightaway.'

Friar Tuck fetched a great crock of wine, and it was poured out for the visitors and Robin.

Robin held his cup high. 'Before you drink, a toast!' he cried. 'Here's to King Richard of great renown. May all his enemies go down in defeat!'

All drank the King's health, even the King himself. 'Surely,' he said, 'you have drunk to your own confusion. Are not you and your men the King's enemies?'

Robin's eyes flashed. 'We are not! We of Sherwood are more loyal to the King than crooked monks and friars. We would serve him gladly. We would die for him. People like you hide in your abbeys and do not care what happens to our country.'

The King shrugged his shoulders. 'I think you go too far, fellow. As far as I am concerned I care very much about the King's welfare. But do not let us argue. We have paid well for our drink. I have heard that you are among the best archers in the land. Will you show us your skill?'

'With pleasure,' said Robin. 'Lads, set up a garland at the end of the glade.'

Soon they had prepared a wreath of leaves and hung it on a stake in front of a tree a hundred yards away. Six of the outlaws stepped forward, each with his bow. 'Three arrows each,' said Robin, 'and you have to get them all inside the garland. If you miss, then Will Scarlet will thump your head for you.'

David of Doncaster shot first, and all his arrows went through the small space between the leaves. Then followed Much the miller's son, but one of his arrows missed the mark by a finger's breadth.

'Come here, lad,' said Will Scarlet gently, 'and receive your reward.'

Much stood in front of him, his face screwed up and his eyes closed. Will rolled up his sleeve and gave Much's head a punch that toppled him over. Much sat on the grass, rubbing his ears, blinking at the stars that danced before his eyes.

The outlaws broke into a gale of laughter, and the King joined in. Four more bowmen had their turn. Two escaped Will's fist because their arrows flew through the garland, but two had to undergo the treatment that Much had received. They took it all in good humour, and the King was impressed by their sportsmanship.

Last of all, Robin stepped up to the mark, and all fell silent. His first arrow went through the leaves and split a piece from the stake. The second did likewise.

'In truth,' King Richard said to himself, 'I would give a thousand pounds to have this man in my guard.'

Robin shot his third arrow, but the feathers on it were uneven and it swerved slightly to the left in flight. It missed the garland by a good three inches.

A roar went up from the outlaws for it was not often that Robin missed the target. Robin flung down his bow in anger. 'I felt as it left my fingers that something was wrong with the arrow,' he said. 'I will try again, and this time I shall not miss.'

But Will Scarlet, in the same gentle voice, said, 'Oh, no, my master. You have had your three shots, and the last went astray. You must take your medicine like the rest.'

'I do not like medicine,' Robin cried hotly, 'and as I am king in this forest no man may lift his hand against me. Not even you, Friar Tuck, who owe allegiance to the holy Pope, because you are still my subject.' He said to the King, 'But to you, holy brother, who are not one of us, I will give permission to give me the blow that I deny Will Scarlet. Are you strong enough to lift your arm?'

'I may be but a weak friar,' said the King, 'but I owe you something for lifting a heavy weight from my purse. So I will try to knock you down, though I fear your Will would have done it much better.'

'If you succeed I will give you your fifty pounds back,' Robin promised. 'But if you don't I will take from you every farthing you possess. Is that a fair exchange?'

'Very fair,' said the King, rolling up his sleeve and showing an arm so taut and muscular that the outlaws stared in amazement.

Robin stood with his feet wide apart, his body tensed, but not really expecting that the friar would land more than a soft thump on his chest. But to his horror he found himself spreadeagled on the ground, his head spinning, all the breath knocked out of his body.

The outlaws did not dare to laugh, but a low rumble escaped them. For several moments Robin lay still, as if stunned, but at last he opened his eyes and managed to focus them on the friar, who was examining his sore knuckles.

Robin sat up gingerly, groaned, and painfully got to his feet. 'Will,' he muttered, 'give this fellow his fifty pounds back. I want no more to do with him. I wish now I had let you give me your medicine – his is too harsh.'

The King dropped the money into his purse. 'Thank you, Robin Hood. If you should ever want a companion blow I will not charge you fifty pounds – you shall have it for nothing!'

Before Robin had time to splutter a reply there came the sound of urgent voices, and into the clearing ran Little John leading a crowd of excited outlaws. In their midst was a knight on horseback whom Robin recognized as Sir Richard of the Lea, the friend he had not seen since he had given him the four hundred pounds later extracted from the Bishop of Hereford.

'What brings you here?' he asked, puzzled by the commotion.

'Dear friend, make haste!' Sir Richard cried. 'Gather all your men together and come with me to Castle Lea. King Richard left Nottingham this morning with six

of his men, my son among them, with the idea of finding you. I do not know what they intend to do, but it would be best for you not to be discovered. I will hide you in the castle until the coast is clear. Come, there is not a moment to lose—'

He stopped short when he saw the seven friars standing with bowed heads. 'Who are these men?'

'Only some guests we met on the road to Mansfield this morning and invited to drink with us,' Robin said. 'I do not know their names, but one of them has a fist like a lump of iron!'

Sir Richard looked at the tallest friar who suddenly flung back his cowl. The knight flung himself off his horse and dropped to his knees. When the outlaws saw the face of their King they too fell to their knees and there was a horrified silence in the glade.

It was broken by the King. He looked sternly around him before his gaze rested on the bent figure of Sir Richard of the Lea. 'What is this?' he said. 'How dare you come between me and these fellows? How dare you offer your castle as a refuge? Will you make it a hiding-place for the most renowned outlaws in England?'

Sir Richard looked up at the King. His trembling hands showed his fear, but there was courage in his voice. 'Your Majesty, you know that I would do nothing to make you angry, yet I would sooner face your wrath than suffer harm to come to Robin Hood and his men, for to them I owe my life, my honour, everything I have. How can I desert him in his hour of need?' His eyes met the King's unflinchingly.

The King did not speak immediately. He continued to look at the knight with a frown on his face, but there was the slightest twitch at the corner of his mouth. Then he turned to his nobles. 'Is there one of you who would like to say something?'

One of the mock friars moved towards Sir Richard. Throwing back his cowl he revealed himself as the young Sir Henry. He grasped his father's hand and looked the King straight in the face. 'My father has served you faithfully and well, Your Majesty, and so have I. Yet, because his honour is as dear to me as my own, I would join with him in giving shelter to the noble Robin Hood.'

The King's smile broadened. 'Well said, Sir Henry, and well said, Sir Richard. I am glad your son takes after you. I would not have heard you say other than what you did. A man must always stand up for what he believes is right. Rise, all of you, for none of you will suffer harm from me this day.'

The King beckoned Robin Hood to him. 'I hope the blow I gave you has not made you too deaf to hear me,' he said.

'I should have to have no ears at all before I could not hear Your Majesty's voice,' Robin replied. 'As for the blow, I think I have now paid in full for all my sins!'

'Do not talk of sins, good fellow. There are worse things than poaching, and because of your loyalty, your skill, and your love for the common people I give you and all your band a free pardon. No longer are you in danger from the Sheriff of Nottingham or anyone else. No longer is there a price on your head.'

Robin flushed with pleasure. 'I thank you, sire,' he said simply. 'This is the happiest day of my life.'

'But,' said the King, holding up a warning finger, 'I cannot let you roam the forest as you have done. You said a little while ago that you would serve me gladly, and I am going to take you at your word. I want you, Little John and Will Scarlet to return to London with me and become Royal Archers in my special body-guard. As for the rest of your men they may stay here as Royal Foresters and protect my property instead of stealing it, and they will be paid wages for doing so. Outlaws, do you swear that from this day you will serve the King?'

'We swear!' The shout was like a thunderclap.

'Then,' continued the King, 'that brings our business to an end. Now get a feast ready, for I would like to see how you live in this woodland inn.'

That night King Richard lay in Sherwood Forest on a bed of leaves under the stars. Early the next morning he set out for Nottingham, taking Robin Hood, Little John and Will Scarlet with him. Before they left, the three men had to say farewell to their comrades. It was a melancholy occasion. The men had lived, played and fought together for years. It had been a good life, if a hard one, and now it had come to an end. Robin knew that the charm of forest life would always be with him, that he would never forget the sights and sounds and smells of the greenwood, but he realized that it could not have gone on for ever. In the end they would have had to pay the price of their lawlessness. So, with a cheerful face but a heaviness in his heart, he shook the hand and kissed the cheek of every member of the band.

'Farewell, friend. I shall not forget you. I shall come again to see you,' he said to each one. Then he mounted his horse and rode away in the train of King Richard.

The death
of Robin Hood

Life was strange at first for Robin Hood, Little John and
Will Scarlet in the service of the King at his court in
London, but Robin quickly became accustomed to it.
The other two did not find it so easy to settle down.
They missed their friends much more than they thought
they would and, when Robin was not with them, would
make plans to return to Sherwood. But they stayed, out
of loyalty to Robin, for nearly two years. Then Little
John, with the King's permission, went back to Mans-
field and picked up the threads of his old life. Will
Scarlet, who had been driven from home when a lad
because he had accidentally killed his father's steward,

heard the news of his father's death and that all charges against him had been withdrawn. So he too left the court and went back to look after his father's lands.

Robin remained with the King and was his most faithful and loving subject. He won such great fame as an archer and as a fighter in the King's cause that the King created him Earl of Huntingdon. He accompanied the King to the wars in the Holy Land and fought by his side on many occasions. Life was so full that he never had chance to go back to the forest, and the years went by without sight or sound of his former friends. But he often thought of them and vowed that before he died he would see them all again.

Then King Richard was killed in battle in Normandy while besieging the Castle of Châlus, and Robin returned to England alone. Now that he was free and owed allegiance to no man he had a great yearning to fulfil his vow. London was a fine place, but an empty place without the King he had served so long. It was not green and peaceful like the forest.

He sought an audience with King John, Richard's brother and successor, and begged to be allowed to leave the court.

King John, who had always resented Robin's influence with his brother, was cold and unsympathetic. 'You wish to go to Nottingham?' he said. 'No doubt to kill my deer and rob my subjects?'

'No, Your Majesty,' said Robin, his anger rising at the King's sarcasm. 'I wish merely to see again the countryside where I lived so long and passed so many happy years. I have no desire to rob anyone.'

The King decided that it might be a good thing to rid himself of his brother's favourite so, while pretending to be reluctant, finally gave his permission. 'But you must return after three days,' he said. 'I must know what the Earl of Huntingdon is up to.'

'That is a very short time,' said the disappointed Robin.

'If you do not return within that time,' said the King, 'I shall declare you an outlaw again. The audience is over.'

So Robin rode to Nottingham and took a room at the *Salutation* inn for the night. He did not seek an audience with the Sheriff, now a very old man, for although his rank demanded such a courtesy, Robin thought there were too many unsettled scores between them, and such a meeting would not be a happy occasion. He slept fitfully that night, thinking with growing excitement of seeing the forest again, and the next day he set out as early as possible.

How quiet everything is, he thought, as he threaded his way through the trees. It was all so familiar, as if he had only been away a few weeks. Memories flooded through him. It seemed as though each tree, twig and blade of grass was welcoming his return, and the song of birds was like a hymn of joy. He had often trod this path with Little John beside him. Yonder was the river over which he and Friar Tuck had carried each other. So much was the same, but so much was different too, the path choked with brambles, a fallen tree lying across it. And the solitude was unnerving.

At last he arrived at the place where his feet had been leading him of their own accord. It was the clearing where they had lived and spent so many memorable days. He heard the trickle of the little stream nearby, and saw the noble trees circling the giant oak under whose spreading branches he had slept. Now the clearing was empty, neglected, inhabited only by ghosts of the past.

'How could I have left all this?' he asked himself.

That morning he had slung his old hunting horn over his shoulder. It had been his constant companion in the old days, and a longing to sound it again was too strong to be denied. He put it to his lips and blew three clear blasts, and in his mind's eye he saw the forest stir, as it used to, and a band of sturdy men in Lincoln green come from behind bush and through thicket to obey his commands.

By a strange coincidence Little John had that day felt the urge to wander through the forest and had left his home to tramp the seven miles from Mansfield. He had just passed the ruins of the old widow's cottage, his mind full of memories, when the notes of the distant horn fell on his ear. He started, his heart suddenly thudding with wild excitement, then said to himself, 'It cannot be – my ears are playing me tricks, conjuring up the sounds of long ago. I shall be imagining I can see my dear old master next …' He tried to put the fanciful ideas out of his head, but in spite of himself he found that he was walking quickly towards where the sound had come from. 'I shall soon be in the clearing,' he thought, and increased his pace. Then he was running wildly, careless of obstacles that scratched his flesh and tore his clothes.

Robin stood in the clearing, reluctant to move on, glad that there was no one to see the unaccustomed tears running down his cheeks. Suddenly he heard a sound like a wild boar crashing through the undergrowth, followed by a voice as sweet to his ear as a choir of blackbirds. He swung round as the figure burst into view. 'Little John ...'

'Master! Master Robin! Is it really you? Is this a dream?'

'It is I who should ask that! I am real enough, but you – surely my horn must have called up a spirit!'

Little John threw himself down and clasped his arms round Robin's knees. 'Master Robin, how good it is to see you after all these years. Welcome – welcome back to the greenwood.'

Robin drew him to his feet and the two men looked at each other in glad surprise. 'The same old Little John,' Robin exclaimed. 'But your beard is white and there is more of you round the middle!'

Little John surveyed his master. 'Your hair is grizzled and your face more lined, but you are the same Robin Hood!'

Before they had chance to say more the clearing was suddenly alive with men, for the King's Foresters had heard the call and had hurried to the spot to see who could blow notes like Robin Hood. When they had recovered from their surprise they greeted Robin, and the forest resounded with laughter and excited talk. In ones and twos other men arrived and soon the men in Lincoln green were together again, overjoyed to see the man who had held their love and allegiance.

After a while Robin moved away from the crowd and jumped on to a tree stump. 'Friends,' he said, 'I cannot find the words to say how joyful I am to see you again. I realize now how much I have missed you and this beloved greenwood. I came here today as Robert, Earl of Huntingdon. I spent years in the service of King Richard, but for King John I have no love. From this moment I am once again Robin Hood of Sherwood Forest, and those King's Foresters who wish are welcome to join my band of brothers.'

'I wish it!' Little John cried eagerly.

'And I,' said Will Stutely, stepping forward. 'It has been dull on the right side of the law!'

There was an enthusiastic shout of agreement from every man present, and Robin looked them over, recognizing one familiar face after another in spite of the changes that the years had brought. But there was somebody missing.

'Where is Friar Tuck?' he said quietly to Will Stutely.

'Dead, master, some years ago. He lost the heart to live when there was no longer any challenge and excitement, and when he had no excuse for a fight. He is buried here in the forest, and I will take you to see his grave.'

Robin was silent for a moment. 'I cannot see Much, the miller's son,' he said. 'Surely he too—'

'No, Robin, he lives and we see him sometimes. He fell in love with Molly from the *Black Swan* and now keeps the inn. But all the rest are here, and ready to follow you as of old. Now, master, I think it is time for a celebration. Come, lads, we are poachers again!'

The news that Robin Hood and the outlaws were together again soon spread through the neighbourhood, to the great joy of the common people, who were even more oppressed than they had been in the old days. It was not long before King John was informed, and he flew into a rage. 'Not only has Robin Hood defied my orders to return to London, he has again put himself at the head of a band of cutthroat robbers,' he fumed. 'He *must* be captured and put to death.' He sent word to the Sheriff of Nottingham that outright war should be waged against the outlaws, and waited impatiently for news of the outcome.

The Sheriff was in duty bound to obey the King, but secretly he feared another encounter with Robin Hood and made only half-hearted attempts to round up the outlaws. Time went by with no news of their capture, and the King decided to take matters into his own hands. He sent for Sir William Dale, a knight of his court who knew Sherwood Forest well and had, many years before, been head of the King's Foresters. 'Take a hundred of your finest bowmen and go to Nottinghamshire,' the King commanded him. 'Bring Robin Hood back to London as your prisoner, if you will, or leave him dead in the forest. I do not mind which.'

The hundred strong army set out for Sherwood. Robin had long suspected that King John would seek revenge and was well prepared for Sir William. But, as always, he had no wish to engage in battle and risk the lives of his men. All he wanted was to live in peace with his friends. For a while they were able to evade an open encounter but at last Robin realized that they could not remain hidden in the depths of the forest for ever.

'Little John,' he said one day, 'no one can say that I have ever turned my back on danger. For my pride's sake I must do battle with the King's army that surrounds us.'

'Because it was your wish, the men have been willing to be patient,' Little John replied. 'Now I think it is time to show Sir William who has the better right to be here. The men think as I do, and are willing to risk all hazards.'

'Well said, Little John. We will send our unwelcome visitors back to London, and bury those who are too dead to go.' Robin, relieved at coming to a decision, was impatient for action. 'Get the men together and we will plan our strategy.'

The next day Robin and his men waited for Sir William's army to make another sortie into the forest, lying low in ambush in the tall bracken, behind bushes and high in the branches of densely-leaved trees. Sir William, at the head of his men, strode purposefully along the broad path. He halted as Robin Hood stepped in front of him. He stiffened, but otherwise made no move.

'Good day to you, Sir William,' Robin said. 'Who are you looking for so deep in the forest?'

The knight looked coldly at the outlaw. 'Robert, Earl of Huntingdon,' he said, 'I charge you in the name of King John to surrender and return with me to London to stand your trial.' Behind him his bowmen had quickly strung their bows. He put up a hand to restrain them. 'Have you anything to say?'

'I will never surrender, Sir William, even if I were alone with you and your soldiers. But I am not alone!' With the speed of a hare Robin darted behind a tree and the sound of his horn brought out the outlaws from their hiding-places.

The battle that followed was fierce and bloody. Robin's men, with their knowledge of every twist and turn of the forest paths, every rise and dip in the ground, every tree and bush, had the advantage from the beginning. The knight's men were bewildered by the sudden appearances and disappearances of their opponents and felt as though they were shooting at ghosts. All the men on both sides fought bravely, but it was not long before Sir William's men were routed. Sir William himself was wounded early on by a well-aimed arrow from Little John. Leaderless, and in complete disarray, the men from London fled, leaving behind them many of their comrades either wounded or dead.

Robin felt little joy in the outlaws' victory. They buried the dead and allowed the wounded to go free, but there was no rejoicing, only a feeling of relief that the forest was now free from those who would have turned them out of it.

That night, resting under the oak tree, Little John

noticed how quiet and pale Robin was. 'Do not fret, master,' he said. 'I know you are upset at the senseless butchery of war, but you did not seek it. It was forced on you.'

'I know that, Little John, and I will not brood over it. To be truthful, I think I am sick of a fever. My head is spinning, and all my limbs are aching. Perhaps I am too old for such excitement—' As Robin spoke his body slumped and he fell backwards in a faint.

Alarmed, for Robin Hood had never been ill before, Little John called Will Stutely, and they lifted him up, laid him on his leafy bed and covered him with a deer-skin blanket. They chafed his wrists and moistened his lips with water, and soon Robin opened his eyes. He gave a wan smile. 'I shall soon be well,' he whispered.

But during the next three days Robin made no progress, though Little John did everything he could think of to bring back colour to his cheeks and life to his limbs. On the fourth day Robin roused himself a little and said, 'I feel a little stronger, but I shall not get rid of my fever until I have been bled. I need to lose some blood to get back my energy.'

'I will send for a doctor,' Little John said.

'No,' said Robin, 'for there is no one near here we could trust. I have a cousin, the Prioress of a nunnery, near Kirklees in Yorkshire. She is skilled in medicine and will know what to do. She owes me a debt, for I persuaded King Richard to make her Prioress. Take me to Kirklees, Little John.'

Leaving Will Stutely in charge of the outlaws, Robin and Little John started a long slow journey to the next county. Robin needed to rest often and when they arrived at the nunnery he was very tired and feeble.

The Prioress welcomed her cousin with seeming pleasure, but she was greatly disturbed when Robin told her how he had given up his earldom and gone back to Sherwood, and how King John had turned against him and had sent Sir William to capture him. She thought that, with Robin in such extreme disfavour, her own position was threatened. The King might depose her, for it was his brother who had put her in charge of the nunnery. 'But if,' she said to herself, 'anything were to happen to Robin Hood, surely the King would be grateful?'

With a false smile she said, 'You were right to come to me. I will make you well,' and she led him up the stone stairs to a bare room beneath the eaves of a round tower. 'You will be safe here,' she said, and added to Little John, who had followed them, 'He must be alone, he needs complete rest and quiet. I shall bleed him soon, and I will let you know when you can take him back to Sherwood.'

Little John reluctantly obeyed the Prioress. He did not like her, but he had no reason to be suspicious of her intentions. After all, she was Robin's cousin, she would surely do him no harm. He left the nunnery grounds and sat down under a tree outside the gate, where he could see the tower, and as patiently as possible he waited for news of his master's progress.

Robin lay on a bed in the small bare room. He was too weary to take much notice of what the Prioress was doing. She bound his arm tightly and with a knife she opened an artery and let the bright blood flow into a basin. Robin sighed and closed his eyes. Soon he would be better ... Quietly the Prioress stole from the room and locked the door behind her, leaving her cousin to die slowly.

When Robin opened his eyes, some time later, he saw the blood still trickling from his arm. He felt very faint. Surely, he thought, I have been bled enough. Why did not his cousin return and bind up the wound? He would die if he did not get attention soon ... He gave a faint call for help, but knew that nobody could hear. He tried to get off the bed and stand up, but he fell to the floor. He crawled over to the door and pushed at it. It was locked. Then the truth dawned on him. The Prioress had betrayed him and had deliberately left him to die ...

He was too weak to staunch the blood himself. The slightest effort brought lights before his eyes and a drumming in his ears. He felt his senses beginning to slip away. 'If I am to die, would that I had Little John by my side ...'

With his last remaining strength he dragged himself to his feet and staggered to the slit window. 'Will Little John hear my call?' he wondered. His horn felt as though it weighed a ton, but he managed to lift it to his lips. The sound was thin, feeble, a ghost of the blast he had once been able to muster. He scarcely heard it himself – nobody else would. He slithered to the floor and gave himself up to despair.

Little John was getting more and more anxious. All

this time, and nobody had come to tell him how Robin Hood was. He paced restlessly up and down, glancing up at the tall tower and wondering what was going on behind those thick walls. Suddenly he pricked his ears up. There had been a sound – the cry of a sickly calf perhaps, or the call of a mournful bird. Or was it a hunting horn – Robin's horn! But Robin would not blow his horn like that unless – unless it was with his dying breath …

Little John sprang into action like a wild horse released from its fetters. He bounded through the gates and across the courtyard to the tower, and took the steps three at a time. 'I'm coming, Robin!' he cried. The door at the top was locked. He threw himself against it with every ounce of power he possessed, oblivious to the pain that streaked through his shoulder. With a crash it flew open, and he saw Robin Hood lying on the floor beneath the window, his eyes closed, scarcely a breath coming from him.

'Master!' He stooped down and gathered Robin in his arms. 'Who would do this to you? What villain would kill my gentle Robin? The woman will pay for this with her life – I will burn the place down – I will—' He looked wildly around as if to find the Prioress already there, waiting to be punished.

'No, Little John.' Robin's whisper was so quiet that Little John had to put his ear to his lips. 'We have never hurt a woman yet. I cannot let you do so now. My cousin has betrayed me. The knowledge of that must be her punishment.'

Little John was tearing a piece from his shirt to make

a bandage. He wrapped it round the open wound and stopped the blood from flowing. 'There!' he panted. 'Soon you will begin to feel better.'

'No, Little John, too much of my life's blood has already ebbed away.' Robin's eyelids flickered, and he gave a shuddering sigh. 'I shall never see the forest again – nor all my good friends. Thank God you are with me as I leave this life …' His voice trailed away to nothing.

Little John thought the end had come. But all at once a spark of life seemed to return and blazed into a brief bright flame. 'Help me to stand up, dear friend.'

Little John put his strong arms around Robin and lifted him to his feet.

'Hand me your bow and choose the fairest arrow from your quiver.' Robin gritted his teeth, hung on to Little John and pointed the bow at the open window. 'Where this arrow falls … there dig my grave … lay my bow at my side … and, Little John, see that my grave is always green …'

The arrow flew through the window, and Little John followed the arc it made and saw where it fell to earth. His eyes filled with tears. 'I will obey, master. But, oh, Robin, do not leave me …'

But Robin's body had slumped in his arms. Robin Hood, gentlest of outlaws and stoutest of friends, was dead.

Little John found Robin's last arrow beneath a tree in the wood, and in that spot he buried him, with a green turf at his head and another at his feet and his good bow beside him. 'I will never forget you, Robin,' he said, as he left the graveside and prepared to make his sorrowful way back to Sherwood.

Nor did he, nor those who came after him, and the stories of Robin Hood's great deeds were handed down in song and story through the ages, so that his spirit still lives in the forests where he and his friends roamed dauntless and free.

Some more about outlaws

Highwaymen and Outlaws 40p
John Gilbert

Here are the exploits of all the best-known outlaws and
highwaymen, from Captain Hind's ambush of Cromwell to the
Great Train Robbery of 1963.

Pirates and Buccaneers 40p
John Gilbert

Read the true stories of twenty-four of the infamous pirates who
have made history with their dash and lawlessness. Such ruthless
and bloodthirsty captures can never cease to shock and fascinate.

Bushrangers Bold! 20p
Frank Hatherley

True and thrilling stories of Australia's legendary outlaws.